12 NIGHTS BEFORE CHRISTMAS

THE ASYLUM ADVENT COLLECTION

JACK STEEN

This advent collection is solely dedicated everyone in my VIP Addicts Group.

I only created this for you, because of you.
You all rock and if I'm ever drunk enough to invite you all to my pub, the round is on me!

Special shout out to Terry Schott and Olin Lester for offering free books to those who joined in my Holiday Advent Event in the group.

Let's do it again next year, shall we?

CONTENTS

SO, WHAT'S NEXT?

You're a greedy lot, aren't you? (insert smile because … well, the more you want, the more I'll create, basically).

I'm working on the next Asylum Confession book (and other books too). If you can't wait - join me over on my Patreon account - www.patreon.com/jacksteen where I share monthly confessions - which means you get one confession a month to read before everyone else.

And… if you have a confession you want to share anonymously, I'd love to hear it and share it on your behalf: https://jack steenbooks.com/dailyconfessions/

INTRODUCTION

You think Christmas gets easier when you work the night shift?

It doesn't.

People assume holidays don't reach this floor. They're wrong. December shows up whether the patients are ready or not.

Think of this as an Advent calendar — not the cheerful kind with chocolate and little doors.

This one opens on confessions.

Real ones.

The kind people only give when they've stopped pretending they'll see January.

Twelve nights.

Twelve patients.

Twelve stories that never made the news in a way that mattered.

These were first introduced to my VIP Addicts group during the Asylum Advent Event.

Welcome to the **12 Nights Before Christmas — The Asylum Advent Collection.**

Take a breath.

December gets deeper from here.

NIGHT 1: MARJORIE

MARJORIE INTRO

You work nights long enough, you start to recognize the ones who aren't afraid of dying — just afraid of remembering.

Marjorie Hales came in with frostbite scars and a court record the public pretends to understand. Neglect, infant death, hypothermia. The kind of case people reduce to headlines because it keeps their hands clean.

But Marjorie didn't talk about the cold the way the report did. She talked about warmth. How fast it arrived. How she trusted it. How much it cost.

There's always one patient every December who makes me rethink the whole job. She was mine this year. A woman who made one terrible choice trying to survive one terrible night.

So pour something steady — cocoa, coffee, doesn't matter — and settle in.

This is Night One: Marjorie Hales.

The woman who learned warmth can be just as dangerous as cold.

CHAPTER 1
JACK

People rarely sleep on this floor in December unless they're already in a coma. It may be known as the Death Ward, but during the holidays, there's a jovialness to the crew that I don't try to kill.

Between Ike and the day crew, this floor looks jolly holly. Tonight, Ike has taped ankle-high lights along the baseboards, and someone else taped paper snowflakes along the wall. Someone hung a wreath on my door, the one with the black ribbon braided through it.

Personally, I like it. I plan on adding some skulls next shift.

We have only one patient on the floor tonight. Marjorie. We set her in a corner room with the window that has the least amount of draft. She was given soft restraints, two fingers easy beneath each band.

Her chart doesn't say much. Marjorie is one of those good patients. They kept her in the nursery, and when you hear her story, you'll understand why.

In her room, I take inventory of my patient. She has amputation scars on her hands and looks quite ragged. She has a food tray beside her bed with only a cup on water on it. I turn the cup handle to her good hand, and she gives me a small smile.

"Doing okay?" I ask.

She nods. "Could be a little warmer, though. Any help with that?"

I already placed a warm blanket on her legs shortly after she arrived. I add another now. "We can do warm," I tell her.

"Thank you. Warm puts me in a mood for a bedtime story."

"Music to my ears."

I leave to go grab some blankets. One, I add on top of her, and the other, I place behind her. The way she sighs, it's exactly what she needed.

I adjust the straps on her wrists and ankles to give her a little more slack. "Where does your story begin?" I ask her.

She turns her face toward the window covered in frost then toward the door. A smile blooms on her face, and I could have sworn she saw someone she recognized, except there's no one standing there.

"At the door," she says finally, looking my way. "Are you ready?"

CHAPTER 2
MARJORIE

We lived in the woods in a small cabin everyone forgot about. It was the middle of winter, and my husband had gone into the city to find work, so I was alone. I wasn't scared, though. We had neighbors who would come by to check in regularly.

I mentioned the cabin was small, right? It was small and drafty and not a place you want to raise a baby in the middle of the winter, yet it was home. I grew up in something similar, so I understood the rules of winter in the woods. There, you don't measure time by clocks when snow fell. You count by fingers. If you can still feel them, you're fine.

My baby, Eli, was young, too young for winter. I helped raise my siblings during the winter, so I knew the tricks—steam, blankets, and patience, all three on repeat.

A week after my husband left, Eli got a cough that sounded like paper tearing. Something inside me died every time I heard it.

I remembered the things I needed to do—steam, blankets, and patience. I made us a nest near the stove with the mattress and all the blankets and clothes we had, and I kept melting water on the stove.

I would boil water and hold him where the steam filled the air.

I sang all the time to help drown out his cries. Sometimes it helped but not all the time. It hurt to hear him cry. That cry has embedded into my soul, and it's all I hear now. I hope soon it will end, and I'll be with him and only hear his laughter.

One night, his coughing was so bad all I could do was pray.

The knock surprised me. *Knock, knock.* Pause. *Knock, knock.* It wasn't neighbor loud. It was polite and subtle, the kind of knock you open for because you were taught to be polite too.

I opened the door. A man stood there, except he wasn't quite a man, He was more an angel. He glowed. Believe me or not, he lit up like a candle, steam curling off his edges.

"You shouldn't be out," I told him.

He didn't answer. At least I don't remember him speaking out loud. I do remember being told that no child should suffer the cold. I swear he said it, but maybe he said it only in my mind.

He stepped into the cabin, and heat came with him. The walls stopped their little shivers. Eli's cry lost its teeth. I felt instant warmth wrap around me, and it was like heaven. I retrieved a bottle that I had been warming on the stove and put the bottle to his mouth. He took it.

The angel looked at me and pointed toward a chair. He didn't say anything again, but I understood what he wanted. He wanted me to sit, so I did.

If an angel stood in front of you and told you to do something, you do it.

Eli finished his bottle and grew sleepy in my arms. Not once did he cough. I believe that was a miracle from the angel.

It grew so warm inside the cabin that it was getting hard for me to keep my eyes open. He told me to sleep and said he would keep Eli warm while I did. I crawled onto the bed, underneath the fort of blankets and sweaters, and I slept like I was allowed to.

I remember feeling like I was being held. Maybe I was. Maybe it was God who held me.

They say my neighbors came because the chimney went quiet.

The door was stuck, and they had to shoulder their way in. They found me on the floor, covered in quilts with Eli in my arms. The stove lid held a ghost of heat. Proof, I thought, that he'd been there.

CHAPTER 3
JACK

I take a look at Marjorie's chart and see words like *severe hypothermia, paradoxical undressing, and warmth hallucination probable.*

She doesn't argue with me. "The angel told me to rest," she says. "You don't tell an angel no."

Her hands move under the blanket, the absent rocking motion mothers do even when the weight is a memory.

"Did you add anything to the bottle?" I ask.

She shakes her head then stops halfway. A memory crosses her face, one that seems to surprise her.

"I had a little whiskey," she says. "My mother used to rub it on the babies' gums. I told myself just a little for warmth. Warmth travels faster in a small body, I thought. I thought I was being good."

There's a line between confession and remembering. She's standing on that line, so I don't push.

CHAPTER 4
MARJORIE TO JACK

Winter has rules. Keep the ashes from the lip. Stack wood within easy reach. Stand your back to the door when the wind gets rude.

I followed them the way I should in order for us to survive. My husband promised not to be long, but he lied. He never came home. Never came to see me. Never came to say goodbye.

I refuse to say his name. He chose to be erased, so I'll honor that.

I made lists in the dead of night when I couldn't sleep, lists of things I needed to fix and things I needed to do. I needed to fill in the gaps on the window trim and stuff it with anything and everything I could find.

In between Eli's coughing and crying, I would tell him stories. I'd tell him about springtime and summer, how the sun would feel on his skin and how he'd love to pick flowers with me. I told him about the bees that buzzed and the birds that sang and the rabbits that would fill our tummies.

He listened. He slept. He cried and coughed and slept some more.

I'm not sure who cried more, though, him or me.

It's hard on a mother's heart to hear her baby in pain.

CHAPTER 5
MARJORIE

The undertaker came before the law. He tucked a blanket around Eli and promised he would take care of my baby.

I believed him. No one wants to harm a baby.

The law came after. The law, they don't promise anything, but they sure wrote a lot. I will never forget their words—negligence, manslaughter, fit for evaluation.

They asked questions. That was all they did. I tried to answer as many as I could, but my answers were never good enough.

They took me into their station, and I was soon surrounded by church ladies who brought afghans and told me I was forgiven before I asked.

Forgiven for what?

The law asked questions about Eli like people would ask about a stranger's baby. Was he a good baby? How long was he coughing for? Did he cry a lot?

I told him he was perfect. He laughed once, and I believed in God for a minute. Most importantly, he died warm. At least, I choose to believe he did.

If that makes me a liar, then lying is the mother tongue.

CHAPTER 6
MARJORIE TO JACK

I know he died. That's not something I've ever denied. It's how he died I argue with.

The how doesn't really matter anymore, though, does it?

Do you think he was comfortable? I hope he was. I have to believe he was. I have to believe that the angel kept his promise, that he watched Eli for me, loved him, protected him.

God sent me help. Not because I was a bad mom but because I prayed and asked for help. It's not wrong to ask, is it? It's not wrong to believe God answered me, right?

He's here, did you know that? The angel. He's standing in the doorway, waiting. I think he wants to come in, but he's waiting to be asked.

This is your place, Jack. I already invited him into my home. This time, it's your turn.

CHAPTER 7
MARJORIE

Whiskey. We didn't have much left, but we did have some. My husband liked to drink it, but he left a few swallows in the bottle high up in the cupboard.

I forgot about the whiskey. Forgot that I got it down. Forgot that I used it. How could I forget?

I poured myself a small amount, barely enough for a swallow. I gave Eli a little bit, just a few drops in his bottle, just enough to keep him warm and help him not cough.

With the angel there, it was like I had permission. Permission to keep my son safe. Permission to keep my son warm. I asked for permission to sleep without worrying about Eli, and the angel gave me that.

Here's the truth I was never asked—I would do anything and everything again to help my son get warm, even if it was for only ten seconds.

I know that's a confession without absolution.

CHAPTER 8
MARJORIE

I've never quite got warm after that night. No matter how many blankets or warm showers I have, I'm always freezing.

Court was cold in a way I'll never forget.

The prosecutor spoke like I was a drunken liar.

The judge waited like he wanted someone to finish a chore.

The town made me into an example of how hard life could get.

I don't listen to what any of them said then or say now. I choose to listen to the angel. He says I did nothing wrong. He says I protected my child as any mother would.

The court didn't listen to the angel. I'm not even sure the angel would have spoken to them even if they wanted to listen.

They said I killed my baby even though I know that's not what happened.

You want me to say I know the difference between miracle and mistake. I don't. I know the difference between cold and warm. Only one lets you sleep.

My sister wanted me to say it was the devil who whispered in my ear.

The pastor wanted me to say it was temptation.

No one wanted to believe me when I told them it was the

angel. People want to believe in angels, in miracles, in answered prayers... but only when it's convenient to them and for them. But God doesn't always work like that, does He?

CHAPTER 9
JACK

"Is it here?" I ask. I won't look toward the door, but I do feel a presence.

"It? You mean angel." She turns her face toward the door and smiles.

"Does it still need permission to enter?" A shiver runs down my spine, but I still don't turn.

"I don't think it matters anymore." She breathes out all the air left in her lungs. Her exhale sounds like, "Eli." Her face changes, not to peace but to acceptance.

I wonder if she heard his laughter before she died. I hope she did.

I note the time.

The hallway throws a thin gold rectangle onto the floor in the shape of a door open enough for polite ghosts.

Ike taps the frame with two knuckles on his way by, our version of a blessing.

The heater dies, but the room doesn't cool.

On the sheet near her wrist, there's a dark oval the size of a child's palm, the outline of where warmth once rested long enough to say goodbye. It lightens while I'm watching. I don't put it in the chart.

17

Before I go, I tuck in the blanket beneath her heels the way you tuck in babies so they think they're still being held.

I look back to the door to see if I really am alone. There's no one there, but I still feel a presence.

Don't tell anyone, but I thank whoever deserves it—for coming, for leaving, for knowing which was kinder.

Marjorie was just a mom trying to care for her baby the best way she could.

I know you're asking if I believe in angels.

On this floor, anything can happen, and everything has happened, or at least, I think it has. This floor doesn't require belief. All it needs is truth.

Here's what I know. I know a room stayed warm after it shouldn't. I know a mother used the tools she had and was punished for believing permission could be mercy. I know forgiveness is something given to those covered in guilt, and Marjorie wasn't someone who needed forgiveness.

NIGHT 2: ELLIOT

ELLIOT INTRO

Some patients show up already half-gone. Elliot Crane was nineteen but carried the weight of someone twice that. Catatonic most days. Throat too tight for words. Eyes fixed on whatever memory refused to let him age.

They called him a prodigy once. Choir boy. Perfect pitch. The kind of kid churches parade around for Christmas services.

The only record that still matters is one sentence he finally typed:

"I asked God for silence."

People forget silence can come in the wrong form.

Christmas Eve. A nativity display. A choirmaster who never made it home. And Elliot — a boy who stopped singing years before anyone bothered to ask why.

He gave me a truth no one else earned. That's why he's here tonight.

Top off your drink.

This is Night Two: Elliot Crane.

The boy who wanted the music to stop.

CHAPTER 1
JACK

There's a particular kind of quiet that settles on my floor in December. It isn't the *peace on earth* kind. It's the breath people hold when they see the end—their end—finally has come.

Elliot Crane is only nineteen. It's not often I have someone so young up here. It hits a certain way, a different way, when they're younger.

Elliot Crane suffers from catatonia, which is basically a medical word to say the kid can barely move, and he doesn't speak. It's usually a neuropsychiatric disorder.

Before his arrival, I got a call from the warden. Elliot Crane is a special case, and he wants me to offer him a deal. That one took me back a bit. How am I supposed to listen to a confession when my patient doesn't even speak?

"You'll find a way," he said before hanging up.

Find a way. Like it would be that easy. I'm not about to give him a notebook and a pen or a pencil or even a crayon.

Ike is the one with the solution. He hands me an old iPad. "Nothing on here but games and the notes app," he says, "but it should do the trick."

I eye it and sigh. "It'll do the trick."

"Think he'll tell you anything we don't already know?"

I shrug. What we know isn't much. A choirmaster was found on Christmas Eve with his tongue lying in the manger. Elliot Crane was in the choir and apparently didn't want to listen to his abuser sing anymore.

I don't think anyone ever blamed him.

When I enter his room, I introduce myself. Elliot just looks at me.

I set down a cup of ice chips and pull up the chair. "Listen, it's Christmas Eve, so I'll give you a gift if you'd like it. Not sure if you've heard of my deals or not, but if you're ready to close your eyes and never have to live another day like you are right now, I can make that happen."

He blinks.

I set the iPad down on the tray. "You've got a story to tell. I have no idea if anyone has ever given you the ability to tell it, but if you're interested…" I turn the tablet on and bring up the notes. "You tell me your story, and I'll make things easier for you."

He looks. No expression. No response. I know he heard me, he's not deaf, but I have no idea if he'll take me up on the offer or not.

I place the tablet on his lap. I know he can move his fingers but can barely lift his arms.

When I came back an hour later, there are five words typed. *Forgive me for the choir.*

"I'm not a fucking priest," I tell him. "You want your sins forgiven, I can get the clergy up here."

He types one word. *No.*

"Then don't expect forgiveness from me, got it?"

He blinks once.

I'll take that as a yes.

CHAPTER 2
JACK

I prefer the nights in this place. There's an honesty that comes around after midnight that you don't get during the day. If you've been here long enough, you'll understand what I'm saying.

I head back to the nurses station and grab a coffee. This is going to be a long night. Usually, I get to listen to someone when they tell me their story. Tonight, it'll be me sitting in silence while Elliot types.

"Why sit there?" Ike asks. "Just leave the table with him and read what he writes after."

That's a solid plan actually.

I give it a solid hour before I head back to Elliot's room.

He's written more on the tablet.

Not everyone deserves to sing.

Beneath his pillow is a book. I pull it out and realize it's a hymnal—St. Matthew's, stamped in gold foil that has been rubbed down to a bald shine along the tired green cloth edges.

"This special?" I ask.

He doesn't nod. He doesn't shake his head. What he does do is look at the book and not look away. That's as loud as some people can be.

I set it on the tray and open to wherever it wants to. "O Come,

All Ye Faithful." A hymn I've only ever heard sung by people who barely know what faith is until it goes missing.

On the margin of the page, someone drew a straight and thin ladder with five rungs. The pencil had been pressed hard enough to dent the paper.

I leave the hymnbook and the tablet. Twenty minutes later, I come back and check his chart and the lines. Only then do I look at the tablet again.

I don't want to say the name.

Underneath, smaller, he added, *He said not to.*

I sit in the chair by his bed. "Names don't matter here," I tell. "We can call him something else for all I care.

His hands lay flat on the sheet like he's holding a page flat.

"Tell me what you want to be forgiven for," I say. Sometimes, the answer is written in the wrong question.

Wanting him quiet.

Then, on the next line, he writes, *wishing.*

Wishes make people uneasy. Wishing blurs the line between what we think and what we do, but if there's any ward where lines refuse to stay straight, it's mine.

"Don't think I blame you," I say before standing. "Start typing, and I'll be back with a warmer blanket for you."

He doesn't move. Some boys learn to be statues. It's the only way for them to survive in rooms where movement is mistaken for consent.

When I leave, I take the hymnal with me. Not sure why, but I felt like I needed to, and surprisingly, Elliot didn't seem to mind.

Sometimes, permission is agreeing to be lighter for a minute while someone else carries the weight. I guess this is me carrying the weight for him.

CHAPTER 3
ELLIOT TO JACK

I don't like the way sound fills a room. When I was little, it was like a balloon that kept getting bigger, and if you touched it with your nail, everything would pop and make a mess, and you have to clean up with your eyes closed.

We wore red. That's important. They called it a cassock, but it's just a dress with buttons that won't stay still if your hands shake. We wore white over it, and the white made the red look like blood.

He wanted us to sing like angels, but we were boys, and angels don't have to breathe. We did. Still do. We turned colors if we held a note too long.

He would press two fingers to our throat, to the soft part where you swallow, and say, "There. Feel the control."

I didn't want control. I wanted air.

I don't want to write his name. In my head, he's just a mouth. That's not a name. It's a shape.

When I say I wanted him quiet, I mean I wanted a door that would close and stay closed. I mean the kind of quiet where your body doesn't need to tell the truth because it isn't being asked a question that shouldn't be answered.

You understand, right?

Christmas Eve is the worst night to make a mistake.

That night, I didn't pray right. I wanted the lies to stop. I wished the song would stop coming out of him. I didn't think about what happens to a song when you cut it in the middle. I just wanted it to end.

Forgive me for that. Not for what came after. For the wanting.

CHAPTER 4
ELLIOT

I learned early on that music is a test you can fail in front of everyone.

Red cassock, white surplice, hair combed so not strand sticks up. I was nine the first time the choirmaster touched my throat to show where the note should sit. I tried to push the song there, and the back of my tongue would cramp like it was going to spit something out.

The choirmaster said excellence was a kind of prayer. The choirmaster said God was listening for a clean line. The choirmaster said when I swallowed, I ruined the shape of the music and that makes the baby Jesus cry.

I was nine. Baby Jesus was just a doll they took out of a box and placed in the wooden bed that smelled like bleach, so if anyone was crying, it was one of the other boys, not the doll.

It was probably the one whose voice kept cracking. He would have his chin pinched hard enough that it was always bruised. No one said anything about it, not even when he lowered his head so his chin was hidden behind the collar.

"Again," the choirmaster said, and I sang it again and again and again until the word again stopped meaning anything. I learned how to split myself. One boy watched the clock, and one boy kept the pitch clean enough not to be noticed. The first boy hated the second boy. The second boy was a shield the first boy held up until his arms shook.

It wasn't a secret, you know.

Those of us in the choir, we didn't have a name for any of it. There was a room at the end of the hall with a green rug and a lamp with a chain that needed to be pulled twice to turn off. That was the room where we'd get help. *I'm going to help Elliot find the line* kind of help.

Once, in the storage room behind the chancel, I heard a sound like someone trying not to breathe. I knew what that sound looked like, what it felt like.

"Don't be dramatic," the choirmaster said when I finally cried once, soundless, my mouth open like a fish gulping stew-thick air. "You aren't hurt. You're undisciplined."

I never cried again after that.

By the time I turned twelve, I learned how to show up for rehearsal with a body that was just a hanger for red and white and a mouth that could make a note without any skin in it.

The choirmaster liked that. "Pure," he said, but the word felt like a scraped knee.

The first Christmas Eve after I turned fourteen, I prayed, and it was a real prayer, which surprised me. I prayed for the song to stop coming out of the choirmaster.

I didn't pray for death or pain or anything with blood in it. I prayed for silence.

That was the only prayer I ever prayed that was actually heard.

CHAPTER 5
JACK

I've heard a lot of stories from a lot of sick-hearted people.

I'm not going to lie. Stories like this, they hurt the most.

I leave Elliot's room to give him some space to keep writing his story. Guess who's sitting in my office? The man himself.

"How's the chat with Elliot coming along?" He's polite, but there's an edge to his voice.

"What's so special about Elliot?"

We all know where his story is headed—Catholic church, choir master... you can piece it together, can't you? Sure, I want to puke reading his confession, but he deserves an outlet to tell his truth.

"The boy caused a small parish a great deal of scandal, and closure would be a kindness to several parties," he says.

Several parties. That tells me more than I think he intended.

"He's typing away on an old tablet. Not sure who's gonna want to hear this one. Sounds to me what happened was deserved."

"I want that document." His eyes are cold as he stands from my chair.

"Sure."

Nothing else really needs to be said.

He leaves, and eventually, I head back to Elliot with some broth and a spoon.

Elliot watched the steam rise from the soup bowl like a candle with a smile. Ike comes in with another heated blanket, and I lay it over Elliot's legs.

After feeding him, I take a look at what he's written. At the top of the page, he typed a question. *Who will read my story other than you?*

I won't lie to him.

"Does it matter?" I ask. "Think of it this way—you want peace in the afterlife, so tell the story that will give you that. Don't worry about what happens after you tell your truth. I'll take care of the rest, okay?"

He stares at me for a little while before he gives me a subtle nod.

"Are you ready to tell me what happened that Christmas Eve?" I ask him.

If you're going to make things easier for someone at the end, you start by naming the thing that made the middle so hard.

CHAPTER 6
ELLIOT

Christmas Eve was all about rehearsal. The church filled twice that night—early mass for families and midnight mass for the faithful and the tired. My voice sang pure like the choirmaster said, but there was a seam in it that wasn't there before, a hairline crack under the glaze.

There are moments in life when we take snapshots so we'll never forget anything. That night is a snapshot in my mind from the rungs on the ladder the janitor used to hang garland and left leaning against the wall to the side to the candles on the altar. There were four fat ones and two thin ones in brass sticks. The small one in the sacristy smelled like lemons.

The choirmaster's lips were red when he sang. It was always red from the strawberry lip chap he kept in his pocket. The way his lips stretched over the vowels: *O* into *Ah* into *Ee*.

His hands were always moving. Even when the choir was perfectly obedient, they moved, moved, moved, like he was trying to herd sheep already in their pen.

Between the early mass and the midnight one, the choir spent the time in the basement with cocoa that tasted like watered-down chocolate milk and cookies someone's aunt had baked that hurt our teeth when we bit into them.

Midnight came with the sound of a hundred people trying to be quiet. The church swelled, bodies, and coats, and breath fogging when the door opened and let in a blade of winter air. We sang notes that climbed, climbed, climbed, and I carried the line perfectly. I didn't even have to look at the choirmaster.

During "O Holy Night," there was a point where the word *divine* stretched like taffy. I held it the way I'd been taught to hold it, but when I ran out of room in my chest, I stole air as quietly as I could. Not quietly enough, though, because the choirmaster's eyes cut to me then, and his hand made a small motion like a leash being tightened. I dug a nail into my palm and focused on the music.

Afterward, there was a rush of coats and hands. The receiving line of parishioners told us all that we sounded like angels.

A woman with tired lipstick grabbed my wrist and said, "God bless you."

The manger sat where it always sat for Christmas, a little wooden "V" that looked like it could be folded up and slipped behind a radiator in January. The baby's face shone. Someone had put fresh straw in it, which made one of the choir boys sniffle and sneeze at all the worst times.

The choirmaster was in the sacristy humming with his mouth open. He talked to a deacon about pitch and about the one boy who couldn't keep his shoulders still when he breathed.

In the morning, a janitor with cracked knuckles found a tongue in the manger. The janitor believed in signs. He scrubbed toilets for a living. He understood the language of things other people didn't want to touch.

The small tongue sat on top of the baby in the manger. The first scream was a woman's. It sounded like a note breaking.

I went to school after the holiday and counted windows until counting didn't help. I stopped singing out loud. I waited. That was all I did. Wait. Wait for someone to come, to ask my questions, to take me away. When they finally did, they took me someplace with white walls and numbers on the doors, and I would count them every time we walked past.

It made me realize that silence was a gift I'd given to myself. Finally.

CHAPTER 7
ELLIOT TO JACK

They asked me after. Not right after. Later. A man in a tie asked me to walk through Christmas Eve like you walk through a house you don't live in anymore.

"Did you see anyone near the manger?" he said. "Did you hear anything unusual?"

What does unusual mean? Everything is… usual. The church is just a machine that makes noise and calls it comfort, don't you think? I remember the sound of the coat room and the wet gloves and the aunt with the cookies who said she had more at home if we were good boys.

My mother said, "Answer him, Elliot."

I opened my mouth and forgot how.

That was the first time I tried to talk and couldn't.

The tie man said, "It's stressful, I understand."

He didn't. He still doesn't. There's no way anyone understands.

They told us the choirmaster was resting. Later, they said he was resigning for health reasons. Everyone got very good at synonyms. No one said his mouth was different now.

The newspaper said nothing at all about the manger, but everyone knew. That's what a church does best—shares the secrets that matter and hides the ones that can destroy things within the walls.

I stopped going to the choir room. They said I was ungrateful. The priest told my mother there are opportunities you shouldn't throw away. He didn't say what kind.

She cried in the car and said, "We're not like them, El. We don't make trouble."

I felt bad for causing trouble, for my mom having to shoulder every-thing, but feeling bad and doing something about it are two different things. I've learned that.

CHAPTER 8
ELLIOT

The parish tried to fold the incident away like it never happened. The homily was about forgiveness without specifying who needed it. The choir was down one boy who used to stand on the end because he fidgeted less when he could lean against the rail. The choirmaster was "taking a leave." A woman organized a meal train for him anyway.

People have a way of being generous when it cost them nothing but a casserole.

The police came to the school twice then stopped. The tie man came to our house and asked the same questions from different angles. My mother brought me water in paper cups thinking that would help, and when the tie man left, she said thank you like she was apologizing for a dinner that wasn't good enough.

People I thought were friends turned out not to be. The locker room became a nightmare. One would stick out his tongue and mimed cutting it. Someone else would whisper that maybe baby Jesus was hungry while pointing toward my penis. I couldn't say anything, so I'd stare at the tile grout until I sat alone in the locker room.

At home, I would sleep with the radio on low, talk shows instead of music. The voices murmured about weather and traffic and which roads were closed because of an accident and how best to roast a turkey. It was mind numbing, and I needed that.

People stopped speaking to me. They stopped asking me to return to choir. They simply stopped asking questions period. The guidance counselor said I was withdrawn and that I'd eventually speak when I was able to handle the trauma.

The last time I went near the church was because my mother wanted me to say goodbye. She stood in the vestibule and smiled at a woman and told her Merry Christmas. I walked into the nave and stood in front of the manger display like it would tell me something if I stared long enough. The baby was back in its box. The straw had been thrown out. There was a faint outline where the wood had darkened under bleach.

I walked out without touching the holy water. I wanted to be unblessed for a while.

It felt cleaner.

CHAPTER 9
JACK

When I return to my office to give Elliot some time to keep typing, the warden is standing by the nurses station waiting for me.

This must be serious.

"How is Elliot?" he asks.

"Quiet."

I mean, what else would he be?

"The chaplain has suggested a visit."

"He doesn't want one."

"You asked?" The warden raises an eyebrow like I've overstepped.

I probably have, but I don't care.

"Don't need to ask," I tell him. "Do you really think having the chaplain visit is the last memory Elliot wants before he dies?"

"The chaplain is very sensitive."

"So is Elliot."

The warden taps the counter. "This isn't something I need you to fight me on," he says. "Someone very important goes to that church. His son was one of the boys accused before they took Elliot away, and he wants definitive proof that it wasn't his son."

"I mean, the fact Elliot got taken away should be proof enough, don't you think?"

The warden scowls. "The official story is that Elliot had a mental break and was sent away for help. There's no record of him being here, you understand?"

I nod. Hell, yeah, I understand.

"You'll have a record," I say, "but, you won't have his story."

I've already thought about how to do this, how to keep the silence for Elliot in a way that matters.

"That distinction is lost on me, Jack."

"That's why I work nights," I say.

I watch him cancel the chaplain's visit with a sigh that he makes sure I hear. Then, I return to Elliot with more warm broth.

He stares at the steam and lets it brush against his face without blinking, like he's letting his skin learn feel something gentler than breath.

Was that the warden I heard? He's waiting for the truth, isn't he?

I read the note and nod.

I can see Elliot shutting down.

"I have an idea," I say. "You tell me the story you need to get off your chest, and then at the end, we'll create a new note where you tell the story the warden needs. That's the one he'll read."

The only one?

I feel for this kid. Maybe more than I should.

"Is that what you want?" I ask.

His head dips slightly.

"Then that's all he'll read."

CHAPTER 10
ELLIOT

The adolescent psych unit had a hallway that smelled like paper. The doors had windows nobody ever looked through. The interview room had a table with a chip that caught the fabric of my sleeve if I wasn't careful. After the first time, I learned to roll my sleeves.

A woman with a scarf asked soft questions. A man with a folder asked hard ones.

"You're safe now," the scarf said.

"Did you do it?" the folder asked.

"No one will be angry if you tell the truth," the scarf said.

"You're not making this easy," the folder said.

They were a duet that never learned to share a key.

I thought about telling them that the worst part wasn't the night itself. The worst part was what the night did to time. Before, there had been practice and school and cocoa and the cut of air when the door opened in winter and a line of boys in red tried not to sway. After, though, there was a manger and a silence that looked like mercy from far away and hurt when you got close.

I said nothing. My throat was a locked drawer, and I'd swallowed the key.

They asked about the choirmaster's "private lessons."

The scarf looked at the folder like she was trying to teach him a new way to ask a question. The folder pretended not to notice.

I stared at my hand, at the pencil dent on my finger from all those hours copying hymns. The dent was going away, which was both a relief and made me ashamed at the same time.

It felt like cheating to heal.

When they asked about Christmas Eve, I remembered the ladder with five rungs, the tenor who always smelled like after-shave, and the shape the choirmaster's mouth made on the word *night*.

I didn't remember steps that made a straight path to the manger. I did remember the feeling of wanting a world without a certain sound in it, but that was all.

The woman with the scarf gave up before the man with the folder. People like her always stopped sooner. They understood that silence was sometimes a life raft, not a refusal. The folder kept trying because it was his job to make neat piles out of mess.

Eventually, the clock won. There wasn't a neat way to write down what I wasn't saying, so they wrote down something else.

My mother arrived with a coat over her pajamas and said we were leaving. No one stopped us.

At home, she made me toast with too much butter and not enough honey. I ate it so she wouldn't cry.

"We will never speak of that place again," she said, and I nodded.

CHAPTER 11
ELLIOT TO JACK

Do you know the real reason people love Christmas? I don't think it's the gifts. I think it's that it's rehearsed. Everyone knows their lines. They know what to expect. They recognize the songs, the carols, the cartoons, and the traditions.

People find comfort in traditions.

Christmas is a time when you can be someone else for a few short weeks. You can be the hero, the giver, the baker, the do-er.

What I loved the most about Christmas was the songs. I still do even if I can't sing them anymore.

They made me believe in something better, that life could be better. For a little while, singing had made me feel safe.

Without that, I feel homeless in my own body, and I don't like that.

I'd give anything for a voice again. Anything.

CHAPTER 12
ELLIOT

On Christmas Eve after the mass, when the church yawned out people in coats and shoes that squeaked on salt, the manger was left sitting without supervision. The baby looked up at rafters that would outlast everyone.

I remember the choirmaster's hand on my shoulder, a weight disguised as guidance. I remember the lips that were always red. I remember the boys listening without wanting to, the way you listen to rain because it was louder than your thoughts.

A congregation would bless a man without meaning to. That was part of the danger. Everyone loved talent. Everyone loved control if they got to be part of its shine.

I remember watching the baby that was not a baby laying on the straw. My mom looked at the manger scene and believed in miracles. I looked at it as saw it as a stage.

In the sacristy, the choirmaster hummed. In the nave, a boy stopped to tie his shoe. In the parking lot, a mother probably told a child to get in the car or else.

What happened between the humming and the morning is something without a memory. It's a room without a door, a room my own brain won't let me access.

I don't remember an instrument. I don't remember blood the way stories described it.

What I do remember is that afterward, the world sounded different, like it had been padded.

That night, the janitor shouted for the priest. The priest shouted for someone else. Then, someone else shouted for no one in particular. The manger sat in its corner announcing nothing. The baby was still looking up.

Later, when the police called it an incident and the paper called it nothing, when the choirmaster was suddenly delicate and excused, when the parish pretended it was a family eating in silence, I put my hand to my throat and pressed where the fingers used to go.

I felt nothing but skin. It was a relief and a loss.

CHAPTER 13
ELLIOT TO JACK

I'm my mom's only son. All I've wanted to do was make her proud and happy. Her thinking I'm bad... that destroyed my soul, and there's no coming back from that.

I can live with being wrong. I can't live with being bad in her eyes.

He made me sing alone that night. Not all the time. Just when he wanted to hear the part he liked best without anyone else making it messy. He said my mouth did what he wanted. It isn't a crime to say "open," is it? It felt like one anyway.

When I wished for silence, I wanted a room where I could close my eyes and not feel someone's hands holding my head still. I wanted to be a window no one could see through.h

Do I have to write it like they want? I don't remember how it got there. I remember the manger and how the baby didn't look at me or but also didn't look away. I remember the shape of the straw. I remember there was no sound in the church even when there were people talking, and then when there was sound, it wasn't singing.

I am sorry for the wishing. I am not sorry for the quiet that came after. I can sleep in it sometimes if the lights are off and no one says my name.

You said you'd make it easier. Please. I want a night without music.

CHAPTER 14
ELLIOT

My voice disappeared right away. The rest happened gradual. Being unable to move and speak was a death in itself. Eventually, I stopped singing in my head.

For a while, the absence made a hiss, like when you turned off a tap and the pipe kept arguing. After that, the world was very clear, and I heard the small things again—the scrape of a chair leg, the way people breathed through their mouths when they thought too hard.

I thought about the boys who still sung and wondered if any of them appreciated what I'd done. I wondered if the parish knew which hymns hurt but sung them anyway.

I wondered if the baby in the box ever had to keep a secret like the one I had given him.

I stayed in bed until the sheets smelled. My mother would bring me tea and tell me it was okay to be tired.

I wanted to tell her it I wasn't tired, but she wouldn't have understood.

When the doctors told my mother I needed to be someplace that could help me, she cried.

I never wanted to see her cry. I hated that my actions caused her to.

I don't think anyone expected me to end up here. When I first arrived, all I would do was look at the ceiling and wait. I waited for the man with the folder, for the woman with the scarf, for the priest with the smooth voice. The first person who came to see me, though, was the warden.

Apparently, I made a powerful enemy when I cut the tongue out of the choirmaster, and strings had been pulled to place me here where no one would remember me.

I cried that night. That was the last time I cried.

CHAPTER 15
ELLIOT TO JACK

I remember when I first met you, Jack. You were different. Different from all the others I'd ever met.

You made jokes without caring if they came across as insensitive. You took the hymnal my mother placed in my belongings, and without asking if it was important, you used it as a door stopper, almost like you understood what it meant to me.

I've never said thank you for that. I don't know how you knew, but all the same, thank you.

Burn that book if you can. Tell my mother I'm singing with the heavenly choir now, please? That will make her happy. If I can do one good thing with my life, it's that.

CHAPTER 16
JACK

Elliot is done telling me his story.

We open a new note, and he spends a total of one minute writing something I can give the warden.

Interested in what he said? I'll add it at the end.

His breathing settles into a pattern I recognize, the sound of a person who is no longer expecting to be summoned for a performance. The little muscles in his jaw finally unclench.

People underestimate how much your jaw has to do with survival.

I sit with him so he won't be alone when the end came. I put my chair where he can see me if he looks up, but he never does. He keeps his eyes closed the whole time.

Elliot dies in his sleep without the need of any help from me. I pull the sheet up so it barely touches his throat.

"You're off the hook," I say. Basically, I'm telling him he doesn't owe anyone a song.

I save his story for myself and print off the one for the warden.

Here's what Elliot wrote. *My mother believes being able to sing is a gift, but not everyone deserves that gift.*

NIGHT 3: MARA

MARA INTRO

Some of the worst stories start with good intentions. Mara Delaney worked in window displays. Retail world. December pressure. Rules no one respects — especially the kind that keep people safe.

The news called it "ornamental cruelty." They never once mentioned the part about three written reports management ignored. They never said how long she kept the store clean so customers could believe in magic for five seconds.

They didn't see what she saw: a room that wouldn't follow the rules she built to hold it together.

When she got to my ward, she couldn't speak. Throat damaged, mutism kicking in. But she typed. And what she typed wasn't madness — it was a record of a woman crushed under everyone else's expectations.

Don't expect a neat moral here. You won't get one.

This is Night Three: Mara Delaney.

The woman who discovered some rooms only behave until someone stops watching.

CHAPTER 1
JACK

Ike sits at his desk, whistling one of those noxious Christmas tunes that sounds like sandpaper to my ears. I'm about to launch a pen at him to get him to stop when my phone rings.

It's the warden.

"Jack."

"Evening, Warden."

"You've got incoming tonight," he says.

"Anyone special?"

Stupid question because if the warden is calling, then it's someone he's interested in or, more likely, someone he wants something from.

"Mara Delaney."

My ears perk up at that. Mara has been on my list for years, but I wasn't sure she'd actually make it to my floor. I figured someone would have taken her out. She's known to have a bit of a temper and doesn't like being questioned.

"There's a complication, though. She got throat-punched, and the doctors say the damage is permanent, so I need you to think of a workaround."

"That's easy. We've got an old tablet she can type on."

"I don't care how as long as you get it."

"Any particular reason?" I doubt he's going to tell me. He rarely does.

He hangs up. Apparently, the answer is *none of your business*.

Mara Delaney arrives not long after.

I wait until she's set up in her room before I make my way down. I catch her eyeing the crease in her sheet down by her knees, just out of reach so she couldn't smooth it. I leave it.

"Welcome to my floor, Mara," I say. "I gotta admit this is a nice holiday surprise."

Her mouth moves like she's trying to speak, but all I hear are squeaks. She swallows, and I can tell she's in pain.

"No words are necessary," I say as I set the tablet down on her lap. She eyes it with interest. "We made a deal years ago. Still interested?"

Her head tilts.

"I'm not here to beg. If you're not, then I'll leave." I go to take back the tablet.

She places her hand on it, and I take that as my answer.

"You remember what I want?"

She nods.

"If you give me any of that shit you tried to sell me years ago, I'm out of here. Got it?"

When I first met Mara, she came into my med room complaining of a migraine. What she was really doing was eyeing me up, gauging my weakness, and seeing how she could exploit it. It didn't take long for her to realize I wasn't to be played with, and after that, we got along fine.

You're probably wondering what I did to get my point across. Too bad. That's between her and me.

Listen, I never said I was a nice guy or even a good guy, and when it comes to these assholes in this place, sometimes you need to be the tough and dangerous guy to get your point across. Got it?

She nods.

"Tell me something no one else knows, and I'll let you decide when you want to say it's lights out."

A small smile plays on her lips at that.

She glances toward the snow globe that sits on the windowsill.

I can't help but smirk. Who the hell placed that there? It's one of my favorite globes, one I found personally a few years ago. It's a cheap, plastic one with a sleigh inside. Nothing special other than the fact that it's gothic themed with a festive skeleton Santa sitting in the sleigh surrounded by black and red gifts.

Mara has a thing with snow globes, but I'm not sure if seeing that one is a good thing or not.

"That's mine, actually. I brought it in. Not sure why it's in here, though. Want me to get rid of it?" I ask.

She turns her attention back to me and shakes her head. Her eyes twinkle a little, like she's sharing a private joke with me.

I turn on the tablet and open the notes app. "I'm ready when you are. I've got shit to do, but I'll be back in a bit to check in on your progress. Sound good?"

She gives me a small thumbs up then begins typing away on the tablet, one finger peck at a time.

Twenty minutes later, I come back. Have you ever been in a hospital room when someone is dying? There's a smell that you can't quite put your finger on. That's what I'm smelling now in Mara's room. Even the smell of antiseptic and bleach doesn't cover it.

The tablet sits at a right angle to the tray, and she nudges it with her knuckles. The restraints limit her reach, which doesn't make it easy to type. I rotate the tablet so the reach is easier. She gives me a look I read to say *thank you*.

Mara points to something she's typed out. *Is it snowing outside?*

"Funny you should ask," I say. I head to the window and pick up the snow globe. "From up here, it looks like we're in our very own snow globe. Fitting, don't you think?"

She smiles.

CHAPTER 2
MARA

Winter never looked right in our house. Snow turned to slush by the door, towels stayed wet, and the floors never clean no matter how much I mopped. My mother called December *the worst month of the year.* She'd put the tree up late and take it down early so she wouldn't have to watch it shed. Every day, she swept needles into the dustpan and muttered that Christmas was for people who could afford to care.

When she slept through the afternoons, I cleaned counters, dishes, laundry, junk mail... anything that could be put back in order. Order made things quieter and more peaceful. It made me quiet and peaceful too.

At school, they called me particular. I liked the word. I don't think they meant it kindly, but that didn't matter. Particular meant *correct.*

My first real job was at the department store in the wrapping section. Customers brought sweaters or candles and told me wrapping was their least favorite part of the holidays. I told them it was my favorite.

I wasn't lying. There's something about creating the perfect look, the perfect wrapping on something selected specifically for one person. I wanted it to be special. I wanted it to be perfect.

They smiled when I handed the wrapped gifts over like I'd performed a miracle for them.

Maybe I had.

I did such a good job I was asked to help with the display cases.

I did such a good job, I was asked to help with the display cases, and I never loved a job more. A window doesn't lie. It just offers the version you can afford. If I arranged a scarf, a chair, and an one open book just right, people stopped to look and believed they caught a piece of peace they could buy.

Glass has rules. Depth lies unless you control the reflection. A lamp placed just so can erase a seam. A single chipped mug can make everything else believable. When the window worked, the whole scene held still.

Leading up to the holidays was crazy. From Halloween to Thanksgiving and then Christmas, the mall was loud and busy. Depending on the focus of my display, kids pressed their hands to the glass, breath fogging the scene, and the crowd pushed close, expecting something special on command. I stayed late quite often changing the display, perfecting it, but I didn't mind.

Management liked to talk about *magic*. They told me I had the *magic* touch, that I brought the *magic* to the holiday season, that I was their *magic* trick. There were days they wanted me to work my *magic* during the day when the crowds could see me. I hated those days. I hated being on display, hated having people watch my every move, point out suggestions, and tap on the glass to get my attention.

I wore black and kept my hair tight to try to hide. The display was the point, not the maker. I was so tense on those days, but when everything was lined, lit, and still, I could feel my shoulders lower and my pulse slow. Clean. Precise. Order has its own kind of warmth.

CHAPTER 3
JACK

I left her room and headed back to my office. The warden drops by. He looks at the tinsel with a raised brow then takes in the skeleton wreath hanging on my office door.

"Festive," he says.

"'Tis the season." I wait for him to say something else.

He stares at the twinkling tree in the corner and sighs. "How is Ms. Delaney feeling?"

Not going to lie but asking how someone is feeling when they're on the *Death Ward* seems kind of redundant, don't you think?

"Tired, but she's got the tablet and is typing."

He nods. I expect something else from him, but he just taps the counter twice and leaves.

"Odd, right?" Ike asks. He's at the computer, updating some logs but kept his head down while the warden was here.

"Must be bored to come up here himself." I fill my coffee mug and head back to Mara.

CHAPTER 4
MARA

Every year, the theme around Christmas was *Home for the Holidays.* Apparently, it gave off the feeling of comfort, warmth, and family. It's a lie marketing pushes, you realize that, right? What marketing doesn't want is stress, loneliness, and frugality. No matter how I felt about the theme, I wasn't paid to question it. I was paid to build it and sell it well enough that strangers believed in it for the thirty seconds they stood there.

So I built a room. A chair with one worn arm placed where a hand would naturally fall. An unfinished puzzle on the table— seventy percent, no more—because someone stepped away to check the oven. A tree with steady lights. No blinking. Blinking looks needy. Snow that sifted down on a timed chute. Not dumped. Controlled.

The night custodian came through with his bag. His humming was always off-key. His cart clipped the platform. It shifted the star on the tree by a hair. Most people wouldn't even have noticed the tile, but I did.

I corrected it with my thumb, checked the lamp again, and smoothed the afghan over the chair arm so the light would fall exactly where I'd planned. My body settled. That's the thing about control. You feel it land.

But the star had moved once. That meant it could move again, and now that I knew a room could slip, I couldn't look away. It ate at me, knowing I wasn't in control. I hated not being in control.

There comes a point in every window when you should stop, a point where perfection has hit and if you keep going, you'll ruin everything. I knew that point. I respected it. It's the one skill no one gives credit for.

But I didn't stop.

The custodian's small collision had cracked the whole idea. The room felt unstable, like the hinge of a door that was about to fall off, so I did what I always do when the weather threatens order—I put the storm inside glass where it can't spread.

"Perfect stillness," my manager liked to say on walkthroughs. He meant it as praise, but it wasn't. He wanted excitement people could photograph, but I wanted obedience.

I staged the morning. Not with mannequins. A mannequin lies. It always looks like it knows it's pretending. No, I used a person. Held in the world I built. I won't give you the method— there are things you shouldn't learn, and I won't be the one who draws a map—but I will tell you that nothing I did was improvisation. Everything had intention.

Dawn hit the glass. The crowd gathered. They saw the stillness. The silence. The chair that had been "sat in." The snow that fell when I told it to and froze when I lifted my hand. A perfect morning that didn't flinch.

They called it "ornamental cruelty." What I heard was "execution of a promise."

Your warden wants a motive the police don't have. They already have the easy story—the locked door, the platform, the custodian. They have a manager who cried the moment reporters arrived. They have a timeline of where I walked, what I touched, and how long the room had been sealed.

They decided I wanted attention. If I wanted attention, I would have stood in the window holding a sign with my name on it. What I wanted was obedience.

And something else… the part they don't have.

I wanted the store to tell the truth about the shape of its care.

For three Decembers, I wrote incident notes, pages of them. "Secure the floor hatch." "Move the platform six inches to align with the load." "Stop allowing customers to reach over the barrier." "No hands on the star after staging." "Replace the gate key. It sticks." "Camera at the north angle is ornamental. Please correct." "Need second staff after eleven p.m."

No one read a single one. When I pushed, they deflected. "Magic," they said, like it was a substitute for labor. That word means "budget cuts but make it whimsical."

There's something the police didn't ask about because they like stories with one break, not a hundred small ones.

Before that night, I tried everything. I rebuilt the room twice. I restaged the entire scene after midnight. I stayed through my shift and into the next, watching the glass and catching every wobble the custodial cart made. I asked the manager to walk the perimeter with me. He laughed, said it was just a display, and asked if I could add more glitter.

So here is my why, clean and without decoration—yes, I wanted stillness, but I also wanted the people who sold "Home for the Holidays" to admit what it costs to keep a promise.

They wanted charm. They wanted warmth on demand. They wanted a perfect window that behaved every time a child smeared their hand across the glass.

They had no idea what that took.

"Home for the Holidays" is not a theme. It's a dare., and I answered it with a room that finally stopped lying. They didn't like the answer because it stayed still when they asked it to move.

CHAPTER 5
MARA TO JACK

You want the part that isn't in the report. Fine. When the window settled that night, when everything held still, I felt… quiet. Not triumphant. Not excited. Just quiet in a way I hadn't felt since I was a child wiping counters while my mother slept.

People think I staged that scene because I was angry or jealous or trying to be seen. I wasn't. I was tired — tired of watching things tilt and waiting for someone else to notice and tired of being the only person who cared enough to keep the room from turning sloppy.

JACK HERE: She stops typing, breathes once shallowly, and then continues.

There's a moment before a mistake becomes irreversible. Most people walk past it. I don't. I feel it in my teeth. The night custodian hit the platform, and I knew the window was going to fail. Not immediately, no. Fail like a slow leak, the kind that ruins everything long before anyone looks down.

I wanted one thing in my life to stay exactly where I put it.

JACK HERE: Her fingers hesitate. Then she writes faster.

When I arranged the scene, it wasn't about cruelty. It was about truth. The window finally looked like what it claimed to be — still, warm, and intact. People saw the result and recoiled, but they didn't see how many times I tried to fix it quietly. They didn't see how many warnings I gave.

I wasn't trying to make a statement. I was trying to make something hold. Something that wouldn't shift the second I turned my back.

JACK HERE: She looks at me then, her gaze steady.

Is that honest enough?

CHAPTER 6
MARA

The interviews were theater. Everyone in that room had already picked the role they wanted from me. One detective wanted anger. The other wanted confession shaped as performance. A third wanted the "methodical woman who snapped."

They asked their questions like prompts. I answered with facts, and they hated that. Facts don't bend. Facts don't audition.

I told them what I built, when I built it, and how many times I warned management. They kept trying to angle my answers into a story that made sense to them. They didn't understand that sense was the wrong scale for what happened. They needed motive, mood, a beginning, middle, and end.

I needed accuracy.

There's something none of them could hear—the moment the crowd outside the window went quiet.

There's the silence when people don't know what to say and the silence when people recognize a line they aren't supposed to cross.

That morning had the second kind.

For one brief moment, the store finally behaved. No fingerprints. No arguing lights. No tilt. The crowd stood on the other side of the glass and understood the display was not for them. It was complete. They couldn't enter it. They couldn't fix it. A room refused them, and they felt it.

The store's lawyer asked if I was "fixated on aesthetic purity." His voice was smooth, like he practiced making people feel inadequate. I told him I was fixated on the idea of *done*. He said, "Done is violent," with that smug look people get when they think they've said something clever. I said, "Done is merciful." He didn't write that down.

The city liaison wanted remorse on record. "Do you have regrets?" he asked, leaning forward like he was offering communion. I told him yes. He asked me to list them, like regrets were receipts he could file. I declined. He frowned, as if refusing to catalogue sorrow was a moral failure.

But you asked me for honesty, so here it is, the part I didn't give them.

I regret believing a window could keep a promise when the people behind it never would. I regret thinking a stable room could come from unstable leadership. I regret that I relied on written warnings when no one in that building respected anything written down.

And yes, I regret using a human body to anchor the scene when every other anchor had failed. That's the part they wanted me to say so they could tape it up and call it motive, but motive isn't a single sentence. Motive is a progression. A slow erosion. A series of doors people refuse to close until you force them to.

I regret learning too late that most rooms lie about what they cost.

When I stopped answering their questions, they wrote "selective mutism." That was partly true but also lazy. I chose silence because letting them shape my words would have been participating in their version of the story. Breath is placement. Once you place it, you've already lost more than you intended.

I wasn't going to spend my breath making their narrative comfortable.

CHAPTER 7
JACK

People ask why patients can't just talk. They think speech is neutral. It isn't. Talking hands over shape, intention, and pace. Talking lets the room decide what to do with you.

Mara's body wasn't willing to pay that price. Her throat still carried the damage from intubation, each swallow catching on something raw. Add mutism born from exhaustion—not fear, exhaustion—and words became too expensive to waste on anyone else.

The tablet is the compromise. It's old and heavy with rubber corners and kept offline. It's the one piece of equipment on this floor that doesn't pretend to be more than it is. We keep two simple games on it because sometimes the mind needs a break to think.

Her thumb drift toward one of them—falling blocks—but she pauses, pulls back, and opens the notes app instead. A decision has been made to work first, comfort later.

I turn my chair slightly so she knows she has space to change her mind without commentary.

She plays one round anyway, silent and steady, every block placed cleanly. When the board fills, she sets the tablet back down, lines up the corners, and exhales once. A reset. Nothing dramatic. Just a moment where the room eases around her.

"Last part," I tell her. "The piece that's mine to hear."

She nods, small and deliberate, and sets her fingertips on the screen. The kind of movement that means the story is ready, and she's decided I won't mishandle it.

Then she starts typing.

CHAPTER 8
MARA

There's a sentence I will give you that I won't give the warden and certainly not one I ever the store.

It is not a confession that changes what I did. It is a confession that changes the room you put it in.

There was a moment, after I fixed the star and before I built the morning, when I stood with my palm on the glass and realized the window was honest and I wasn't. I had spent years telling strangers that a room could be theirs if they bought a scarf. I had spent years telling myself that I was the kind of person who did no harm because I made order.

The truth is that my order always had a mouth behind it. I wanted obedience because I was tired of asking. That's not aesthetic. That's hunger.

The police thought I wanted revenge. The store thought I wanted to embarrass them. The city thought I was a deranged artist.

I wanted none of those.

I wanted the morning to shape itself around a stillness it could not disturb. I wanted the crowd to have to look at a promise kept and understand it cost more than clearance tags and a manager's speech. I wanted proof that a room could hold. I used a person as proof because the store had trained me to believe people were props if the lighting was good.

That's the part I can't let them have.

They would turn it into a lesson with bullet points and slide decks. They would make "ethics training" modules that teach no one how to keep anything safe.

But you can have it. Your ward keeps people honest.

You asked for my why. Here is the hardest one—I wanted to stop being casual with harm, so I did the most formal harm I could imagine. It worked. The morning behaved.

And now I will do the only obedient thing left. I will accept the end you make easier.

CHAPTER 9
MARA TO JACK

If there is a choice, I want the room to keep its shape. I don't want anyone to talk about forgiveness like it's a coupon. I don't want a song to argue with the quiet. I want the kind of ending a display gets when you've locked the gate, turned the key, and checked the angles one last time. Lights to warm. Air to even. Nothing to tilt the star.

Thank you for not making it magic. Magic is a lie that asks you to clap. You didn't ask me to clap.

If you need words for your file, you can write "She preferred obedience to applause. She understood the cost and paid it. She asked for stillness at the end, and she received it."

Does anyone ever ask you, or do they just assume you'll keep your end of the deal?

I'd like to ask. That way, it's my decision.

Please, Jack? I'm ready.

CHAPTER 10
JACK

A snow globe only calms down after you stop shaking it. Most people never learn that the hardest part isn't the stopping. It's keeping your hands off the glass once you've set it down.

We all decorate the end however we can live with it. Ike has tinsel. The warden has files. Mara had a room that finally obeyed. Me? I have the moment when a patient types *please* and I get to see the smile that lingers on her face as she drifts off.

Mara dies at 2:18 a.m. I bring the snow globe back to my office and shake the fuck out of it. That makes me smile.

NIGHT 4: ARTHUR

ARTHUR INTRO

Arthur Cobb looked like any man nearing the end — tired eyes, careful breathing, hands that kept searching for something familiar. But his story started years before he ever landed on my floor.

He buried his wife's heart under their Christmas tree. That's the part the papers grabbed first. They skipped the rest — the grief, the quiet months before it, the promise he made when he still believed he could hold a family together with sheer will.

Arthur wasn't violent by nature. He was a man who didn't know how to live in a world his wife wasn't part of. So he built a version where she stayed.

Permanently.

He didn't tell the judges any of that. He told me. December does that to some people.

Take a breath and settle in.

This is Night Four: Arthur Cobb.

The man who kept a promise long after it should've been released.

CHAPTER 1
JACK

December makes this floor look softer than it is. Some days I like that. Most nights I don't.

Arthur Layne comes up on a gurney with three bracelets and a thin chart mentioning heart failure, kidney trouble, and old injuries in his hands from pruning shears. I already have his file—murder of spouse, body recovered, confession incomplete.

The warden meets him at the elevators. Not a long conversation and certainly not one I listen to. I wait till I'm motioned over.

"You want a story," Arthur says, his voice hoarse but steady, "then talk to the tree. It knows everything."

The warden leaves but not before he gives me a look.

We place Arthur in a corner room where Ike sets a small potted evergreen on the overbed table. Guess the day crew decided every patient needs a little bit of Christmas in the rooms so every tree has something in it. A gnome. A reindeer, one of those cheap holiday village houses you can buy at the thrift store. I don't mind.

Arthur's eyes the tree and frowns. "Too close to the edge," he rasps.

I move it back an inch. "Better?"

He gives the smallest nod. "Trees lean," he says. "You have to think ahead."

"Never really thought about tree placement," I say. "Night shift keeps me pretty busy."

"You once promised you could make it easier. How?" he asks.

"You know how." I give him a look.

He glances at the little tree instead of me. "You want the truth?"

"If you want to give it."

"You won't like it."

"I'm not here to judge."

He lets out a slow breath. "All right. Then we start where everybody thinks it began."

CHAPTER 2
ARTHUR

I grew up in an apartment that never had a tree. The landlord said pine needles ruined the carpet, and my mother said Christmas was a bill she couldn't pay. We got a cardboard wreath and a tin of cookies off the charity list. That was our Christmas. Not even a plastic tree and no decorations unless they were free. Sure, I made homemade stuff as a kid, but Christmas was never a big deal growing up.

When Elaine and I bought our house, the first thing she said was, "We'll have a tree every year. Real, not plastic." She grew up with Christmas and loved it.

Our house wasn't big, but it was ours. The backyard had one open corner, and my girl wanted to plant a tree there. The soil was hard and full of rocks. I tested it with a spade and hit stone three times before I found a line that eventually gave. She stood on the back step in her coat, her hands deep in the pockets, watching the ground open.

She wanted a Christmas tree, a year-round one that would grow throughout our marriage. She was a romantic, and I loved that about her.

"We could just buy one each year," I said. "Put it in a stand and toss it in January."

"No," she answered. "I want one that belongs to us. One that knows our house."

That was that. We drove out to a nursery past the edge of town. In the cold, she walked up and down rows of young spruces in burlap, reading needles with her fingers. I watched her body tip toward one small tree with a crooked top.

"This one," she said.

"It's leaning," I told her.

"It's trying," she said. "So are we."

We took it home. I dug a hole too big because I didn't know what I was doing and wanted to make up for it with effort. She held the tree steady while I shoveled the soil back in.

When we were done, we stood back. The tree looked thin and nervous. The house looked bigger with something planted in front of it.

"This is it," she said. "First Layne Christmas tree."

"You sure it's not too much work?" I asked.

She shook her head. "We're going to make a promise right now."

I wiped my hands on my jeans. "What kind of promise?"

"That we'll always be home for the holidays," she said. "Here. You and me. No hotel rooms. No splitting time between families. This place."

That sounded simple. It felt good in my chest.

"Always?" I asked.

"Always," she said. "We choose this house and this tree. Every December, we choose each other."

We stood there in the cold, our hands linked, looking at that skinny tree, and said it out loud together. "We'll always be home for the holidays."

I didn't hear the part where "always" would keep needing payment long after she ran out of breath. I just heard a thing I could control.

We kept that promise. Every year, no matter what came up, we stayed.

Her mother invited us to Florida once. "You can come down, escape the snow," she said. "We'll do Christmas by the pool."

Elaine said no without looking at me. "We have plans," she told her. She didn't explain. She didn't need to.

The tree grew the way they do, slow enough you only notice in photos. Each December, I strung lights around it. None of the lights could blink. Elaine didn't like blinking.

"Too desperate," she said. "We're not begging anyone to look."

We stayed home when my brother got married on Boxing Day. We sent a gift and a card. He called it stubborn. I said I didn't care. Elaine and I sat under the tree with hot drinks and warm cookies.

She bought one new ornament each year. Never more than that. "One is enough," she'd say. "We're building a memory, not a store display."

The first was a red, heavy glass heart on a thin wire loop. She hung it in the center of the branches at chest height.

"It looks out of place," I said.

"It's the point," she told me. "It's the center. Everything else can work around it."

We had the usual fights couples have. Money. Schedules. Her wanting to try for a child, me afraid of what not knowing how to parent or how to be a good father. I never had one as an example.

The tree never moved. It stayed where we put it, year after year watching us argue and make up and argue again.

Every December, no matter how raw the year had been, we stood under it on Christmas Eve and repeated the promise. "We'll always be home for the holidays. Here. You and me." We said it together even the years when we were angry.

"Do you ever want to go somewhere else? Just once?" she asked me once.

"Do you?" I asked.

She thought about it and shook her head. "No, but I don't want us to ever resent this."

"I don't resent it," I told her. "It makes you happy, and this is home."

I started caring more about the tree than about the house. I watched for bugs. I checked the soil. I worried about neighbors' kids kicking balls too close.

"You're fussing," she said one day. "It's fine."

"If it dies, what does that mean?" I asked.

"It means we plant another," she answered. "The promise wasn't about the tree. It was about us."

The words went in, but they didn't stick. In my head, the two were the same. Us. the tree, and the fact that we stayed.

CHAPTER 3
ARTHUR TO JACK

Jack, I can see you thinking it. You're wondering when it crosses from love to control. You want a line you can highlight.

There isn't one. It happens the way roots go under a fence—a little at a time.

You see me in this bed, strapped, with that little tree on the tray, and you think he let a plant run his life. That's not wrong, but it's not complete.

We thought about leaving once, of not being there like we'd promised.

Elaine got a brochure from a travel agent. "Christmas in Paris," it said. Lights on old streets. Markets. Pastries.

She put it on the kitchen table and looked at me. "It's just a thought experiment," she said. "What if we were the kind of people who did this?"

"We're not," I said.

"I know," she said, but she didn't move the paper.

I took it and put it in the drawer with the batteries and tape. That night, I dreamed the tree was standing alone in the yard with its lights off while we sat under someone else's decorations. I woke up angry. Not at her. At the idea.

I didn't tell her about the dream. I just got up early and checked the soil around the trunk, like that would fix everything.

You think I'm avoiding the main part. I'm not. I'm working my way to it the only way I know how—in order. You work here. You know what happens when people jump straight to the worst moment. They blow the fuse, and the rest never gets said.

Give me another minute. Then we'll go to the hospital mornings and the last December.

CHAPTER 4
ARTHUR

The year she got sick, winter started early. Cold in October. Ice by November. The tree had grown tall enough that I needed a ladder to reach the top. I liked that. It meant our life had history.

Elaine started getting tired by six in the evening. She'd sit down in the chair by the window and stay there. I thought it was work. Long days at the clinic. Flu shots. Paperwork.

She brushed it off. "I'm just getting older," she said. "We both are."

One night in November, she clutched her chest and sat hard on the edge of the bed. The color left her face in stages. I grabbed the phone even though she told me not to.

"It's just indigestion," she said. "Too much coffee."

We argued for two minutes. Then I called anyway.

In the emergency room, machines took over. Words like "angina" and "blockage" entered our life and never left.

The cardiologist said she needed medication, rest, and monitoring. "The heart can only take so much," he said. "You both need to respect that."

I heard the word heart and thought of the glass ornament, the red one she hung every year. It had survived every year, ever winter. Now, her real heart was the thing in danger.

On the drive home, she looked out the window and said, "If anything happens to me, you have to promise me something."

"No," I said. "Nothing's going to happen."

"I'm serious, Arthur."

"So am I." She turned to me. Her face was pale and set. "If I die before you, you have to keep living. You have to go places. You have to let the promise change."

"The promise is the promise," I said. "We always stay. That's what we said."

"We said it together," she answered. "We can change it together. Right now."

My hands tightened on the wheel. The parking lot lights passed over us in regular pulses. "I can't say that," I told her. "Not tonight."

She closed her eyes. "Then say you'll think about it."

"I'll think about it," I said.

But I didn't.

The months after that were filled with tests, appointments, and pills in little boxes. The tree out back dropped needles like usual. Life split into two tracks—what the doctors wanted and what the tree represented. One was about numbers and risk. The other was about a sentence we'd said in the cold when we had been young and sure.

December came. She was on stricter medication. No long walks. No heavy lifting.

The cardiologist didn't like the cold. "It narrows things," he said.

"You're not standing outside while I do the lights," I told her.

"Don't tell me what to do," she said. Her hand shook when she handed me the box.

I went out and did it alone. The tree was taller, and the ladder felt less stable. My breath fogged in the air. I wrapped the lights in slow circles, checking each loop.

Inside, I could see her at the window. Watching.

When I finished, she came out for five minutes with her coat open, boots unlaced, sweater too thin. She stood under the branches. Her breath came shorter than it should.

"Say it," she said.

"We always stay home for the holidays," I said. "Here. You and me."

She hesitated. There was a shift in her face. Then she said, "Here. You and me."

I pretended not to hear the doubt in her voice.

CHAPTER 5
ARTHUR

It happened three days before Christmas.

We had planned a quiet evening because she was tired. I made soup. She sat in her chair with the blanket and watched some old movie on low volume. Snow had started again outside, light but steady. The tree in the yard stood firm in the porch light, its branches outlined in white.

She put her hand to her chest once, twice. I saw it but told myself it was nothing. We both wanted it to be nothing.

Then she gasped, a sound I had never heard from her mouth. Not anger, not surprise. Something else. She bent forward, her fingers digging into the armrest.

"Elaine?" I called.

She couldn't answer. Her face went gray. Sweat on her upper lip. The blanket slid to the floor.

I grabbed the phone. My hands didn't feel attached to me. I dialed. The dispatcher's voice was calm and trained. I answered questions without hearing myself.

While we waited for the ambulance, I kneeled in front of her. Her eyes were unfocused. I called her name. One side of her mouth tried to move. The other side stayed still.

"Stay with me," I said. "We're here. We're home."

Her gaze slid to the window and the tree outside. Its lights were on. In the reflection on the glass, they looked doubled.

"I'm not ready," she mouthed. No sound. Just the shape of the words.

"You're fine," I said. "Help is coming."

She shook her head just once. Her hand tightened on the armrest and then slackened. Her eyes rolled up. I saw the exact moment the person I loved went somewhere else.

The paramedics did what they do--chest compressions, oxygen, lines, words. They worked on her in our living room with the tree watching and then took her to the hospital. I followed in the car.

In the corridor outside the resuscitation room, time stretched. Nurses moved, and machines beeped.

A doctor came out with the face I have seen on this floor more times than I can count. "I'm sorry, Mr. Layne," he said. "We did everything we could."

I heard other words—cardiac arrest, no response, time of death.

My legs didn't trust the floor. I nodded. I answered questions. I signed forms. I called her sister. I did what widowers do.

They asked if I wanted to see her. I said yes. They took me in. She lay on a bed, a sheet to her chest. Her face looked almost the same. The difference was so small it was cruel.

I held her hand. It was still warm.

"You left," I told her. "We promised we'd always be home for the holidays."

It was irrational. I knew that, but the rational part of me was in shock. The irrational part was clear and sharp.

On the drive back, the house lights looked wrong. The tree in the yard glowed steady. In the windows, my reflection looked like a stranger.

Inside, the room was exactly as we had left it—blanket on the floor, her mug half full, the wreath on the door. My world had flipped, and the furniture hadn't moved.

I sat in her chair. The cushion still held the shape of her weight. My hand went to my chest, to the place the cardiologist had pointed at her.

The promise we had made stood up inside me. It didn't bend for death. It didn't care about doctors. It was as rigid as it had been in the yard years before.

If she wasn't there, how could the promise still be true?

Something inside me answered. "You keep her here. You keep her home."

I went back to the hospital. You know the rest from the trial summaries. I signed more papers. I asked for time with the body. I will not tell you the specific steps. You don't need them, and I won't give them.

I will tell you this, though, that when I carried what I took back through our front door, the house felt less empty.

Out in the yard, the tree waited with snow on the branches and its lights steady.

"We said always," I told it. "I'm just doing my part."

I dug into the soil at the base of the trunk. My fingers were numb, but I worked anyway. I placed what I had taken there in the ground, under the roots, right at the spot where her boots had stood when we had planted it.

"There," I said. "Now you can't leave. You're home for every holiday. That's the deal."

I covered the hole, pressed the earth down, and stood up. The tree didn't move. The world stayed in place.

It felt right. That's the worst part. In that moment, it felt exactly right.

CHAPTER 6
ARTHUR TO JACK

You're waiting for me to say I knew it was wrong at once. I didn't. That came later.

You work here. You see people rationalize all kinds of things. You know the stages—shock, logic, collapse.

Those first weeks, I was proud of myself. I tended that spot like it was the center of the world. I checked it every day. I brushed snow away with my gloves. I talked to it.

"I kept my word," I'd say. "You're still here. You didn't go anywhere strange. You're under our tree."

Neighbors called, brought food, and cried in the doorway. Nobody saw the disturbed earth behind them, or if they did, they thought it was grief gardening.

Do I regret it? I'm getting there.

I need you to understand that when I look at that tree, even now in my head, I don't see a crime scene. I see a promise made solid.

That's the problem. Promises don't know when to stop demanding proof.

CHAPTER 7
ARTHUR

I kept the secret three full years.

The first Christmas without her, I wrapped the lights slower than ever. Each time I passed the base of the trunk, I checked the ground. Nothing had shifted. That felt like approval.

I hung the glass heart in the same place she always had, right at chest height, in the center.

"I know you're here," I said. "We're still home."

Inside, I ate at the table alone. Her chair stayed empty. I set a place for her anyway. It felt wrong not to. It also felt wrong to eat in front of it.

People said I was devoted. They used words like "loyal" and "faithful." The town made me into an example. Husband who stayed. Husband who never left the house over the holidays. Husband who kept the tree lit every night.

That fed something in me. I won't pretend it didn't.

The second year, her sister asked me to come stay with them. "Just for a change of scenery," she said. "You don't have to be a monument."

"I can't," I said. "The house needs someone here."

"What about the rest of the year?" she asked.

I shrugged. "Christmas is different."

She looked out at the tree. "You always were fussy about that thing," she said.

"It matters," I told her.

By the third year, the story had hardened. People started telling it for me. "Arthur Layne," they'd say. "He loved his wife so much he never left. He keeps her memory under that tree."

They didn't know how true that was.

But I started to feel trapped. Every December, the expectation grew. If I left even for a day, what would that mean? If I turned off the lights, what would that say?

I had built a cage and then stepped into it. The bars were made of praise.

One night, I had a dream. In it, the tree was gone. Now, it was just a stump and a raw circle of dirt. The house leaned without it.

I woke up sweating and went outside. The tree was there, solid and whole. I put my hand on the trunk. The bark was rough and real.

"I won't let anyone do that," I said out loud. "I won't let you be moved."

I meant it.

CHAPTER 8
ARTHUR TO JACK

The storm came in the fourth winter. Wet snow. Strong wind. The kind of weather that makes branches complain. I watched the tree all night from the window. The lights swung, and the trunk held. I prayed. No, not to any god I was raised with. Just to the structure itself. "Stay up. Don't fall. Don't betray what you hold."

In the morning, a large limb lay on the lawn. It was torn, hanging by a strip of bark. The heart ornament was still on the intact part of the tree, but lower was off-balanced. It looked wrong.

I went out without a coat. The snow went into my shoes. I sawed the broken limb clean from the trunk, my hands shaking. I thought about burning it, but I couldn't bring myself to. It felt too close to burning part of her. I dragged it to the shed and leaned it in a corner.

Neighbors came by with suggestions.

"You should get a professional in," one said. "They'll tell you if it's still safe."

"I can see it's safe," I answered.

"You should think about taking it down," another said, "before it hits the house."

My jaw clenched. "The tree stays," I said.

They had a meeting without me. I know that now because small towns keep nothing private. They talked about property values and risk and my behavior.

A woman from the neighborhood association came to the door with notes. "We're worried," she said. "You've made the yard into a shrine. You're not maintaining it properly. If something happens, there could be issues."

"I maintain it every day," I said. "Better than anyone else would."

"You're very attached," she said as if that were a disease.

I didn't let her in. I didn't argue. I just closed the door.

She came back a few nights later. She probably thought I was sleeping or gone for the night since she couldn't see my car in the garage. I don't know what happened, what came over me, but when I saw her and her husband carrying a chainsaw, something came over me.

I don't need to tell you what happened, but I made sure neither one of them would ever return, and I buried them in the back. No, not under the tree. Not with my wife.

From then on, I watched not only the tree but the people watching it. I felt under siege.

They saw devotion and called it unhealthy. I saw a promise and saw them trying to break it.

I started sleeping in the chair by the window. I could see the tree from there. I was sure someone else would come to take it down, to take her away from me. The house felt like a guard post.

CHAPTER 9
ARTHUR

The pressure built over months. Letters from the association. Notes from the city. "Concerns about safety." "Liability." "Mitigation."

No one ever came about the missing couple.

I'd get phone calls when I wouldn't respond to the letters. They offered to trim it. To cut it back. To make it "manageable."

"I'll do it," I said. "I've done it for years."

But they didn't trust me. They trusted a line in a rule book that said large trees near houses were a risk. They trusted insurance adjusters. They trusted people who had never stood in the cold and promised anything to anyone.

A city inspector came by with a clipboard and a hard hat. He walked around the tree, measuring angles I had never thought to measure. He poked the soil with a metal rod.

"It's close to the house," he said.

"I know that," I answered.

"Roots could affect the foundation," he said.

"Roots hold things," I answered.

He made a note. "We recommend removal," he said. "We'll send you options."

After he left, I stood under the branches. The lights were off. It was daytime. The tree was just wood and needles and weight.

"I won't let them move you," I said. "We said always. I meant it."

I knew that if they took the tree, they would take her with it. Whatever I had buried there would be disturbed and dug up, the promise would be broken in the ugliest way.

I couldn't allow that.

In my head, the options narrowed.

Sell the house and move the tree? Impossible. No one would move it the way it needed to be, and if I left, the point of the promise collapsed.

Fight the city? But I knew how those battles go. I had seen it with my brother and his zoning problems. I would lose.

Make sure no one else ever decided its fate and those who tried regret it? This was the only choice I could make.

CHAPTER 10
ARTHUR TO JACK

You know from the record that I sabotaged equipment. You know I threatened a contractor. You know he reported me. You know the confrontation escalated and he ended up being buried in my backyard too.

What you don't know because I never said it in court is that the moment I pushed him, the moment he fell, I looked past him at the tree.

It stood there, unchanged. It had outlasted my wife, and it would outlast me. The man on the ground was another person trying to rearrange the structure of my life.

I didn't see him as a person. I saw him as a force.

By the time the sirens came, it was too late. Too late for him and too late for me. The city got what it wanted anyway. They cut the tree down as part of the "recovery."

They saw the part of the yard that had been disturbed and dug it up. When they found the bodies, they tore apart the whole yard, expecting to find more.

You've read the reports. You know what they found when they dug up the tree—a box with a jar of alcohol. Inside that jar was a heart.

Her heart.

CHAPTER 11
ARTHUR

The trial was about the man I pushed. It wasn't about the promise. Not really.

The prosecutor painted me as obsessed, unstable, dangerous. I was. The defense painted me as grieving, overwhelmed, provoked. I was that too.

They asked why I never told anyone about what I put under the tree. They called it desecration. They called it an indignity.

They asked if Elaine would have wanted it. I said no. They asked why I did it anyway. I gave them a line about shock and poor judgment. They wrote it down.

What I didn't say is that for three years, that spot in the yard felt more honest than any graveyard rectangle would have. It was the only place that matched the shape of the promise we had made.

I didn't tell them that on quiet nights, I could stand by the trunk and feel calmer than I ever did in a church.

I didn't tell them that every time I thought about moving, my chest tightened and I saw myself leaving her behind in the soil.

I didn't tell them that when they dug up the box that held her heart, it felt like they were pulling out the foundation of my life.

Those are not things courts know what to do with.

They sentenced me. Years. Transferred me to the prison hospital when my own heart started to fail.

They called what I did monstrous. I don't argue with that. A man who uses a body to fix a feeling is not good. But I want it on record that I did not do it to hurt her. I did it because I could not see any other way to keep my word.

CHAPTER 12
JACK

On this floor, the stories tend to end the same way. Breath shortens. Machines get busy.

Arthur's kidneys were failing. His chest hurt with every shallow breath.

I check his restraints. Two fingers under each. No rub marks. I adjust the blanket so it doesn't pull at his shoulders.

"Thirsty?" I ask.

He nods.

I lift the cup and guide the straw. He takes a small sip and holds it in his mouth before swallowing.

"You got what you needed?" he asks, his voice thin.

"I have what I can live with," I say. "Anything you want me to leave out?"

"Don't make me sound noble," he says with a sigh. "I don't deserve that. Just… make it clear I believed I was doing right. Then make it clear I was wrong."

"I can do that."

He looks at the little tree. "Will you take it and care for it? Water it? Watch it?" he asks.

"Yes."

"Even if it doesn't need it," he adds.

"It'll be looked after."

He closes his eyes. "Good." His chest moves slower. His fingers twitch once against the bed rail. "Do you think promises mean anything after we die?" he asks, not opening his eyes.

"I think it doesn't matter anymore to you. To the other person, the promise probably means everything."

"Is there a way to put them down?"

I look at the monitors, at the numbers trying to make life into a graph. "Sometimes," I say. "Sometimes the body does it for you."

He gives a dry laugh that turns into a cough.

We sit in the dim room, the baseboard lights low, snow tapping the window in small, regular touches. The wreath in the hall cast a faint shadow across the doorway.

I stay until he's gone.

CHAPTER 13
JACK

Arthur's heart stops beating at 5:25 a.m.

I take the little evergreen to the nurses station.

Ike raises an eyebrow. "Arthur gone?"

"He asked us to water it."

Ike nods. "We'll keep it alive until the spring and plant it out in the garden."

I think about Arthur's yard and the hole under the real tree. The promise that turned into a crime scene. The way the town loved his devotion until it scared them.

Some promises outlive the people who make them. They don't know when to stop demanding payment.

On my break, I water the little tree. It didn't look thirsty, but I did it anyway.

NIGHT 5: MILO

MILO INTRO

We get all kinds in here — but the ones who grew up learning how to fix things are always the hardest to sit with. Milo Brandt came from a toy shop where his father repaired every broken wheel in town. The man was a local saint. That's how the papers wrote it.

Milo was the kid sweeping the floor behind him. Invisible unless something went wrong.

A game he invented killed a child. A fire he set wiped out the shop. Prison took years. Cancer took his voice. By the time he reached my ward, all he had left were hands that still moved like they remembered sandpaper and old hinges.

He didn't want forgiveness. Just accuracy.

If you've ever been in a room built by a man who felt unnecessary, you'll recognize every line he gives you.

Pull up a chair.

This is Night Five: Milo Brandt.

The toymaker's son who learned too late that some repairs are just another kind of damage.

CHAPTER 1
JACK

The day shift put a donation bin at the nurses station. It's almost full now—cans, boxes, a few toys. The idea is to send it all to a church that hands out Christmas hampers.

My mother keeps sending bags in with my name on them. I drop them in the bin. She's the one with the soft heart. I'm just the son who answers her texts. I add some grocery gift cards so I can say I did something myself.

Someone dropped a little plastic drum into the bin. It keeps ending up back on top because Ike likes to play with it. I tell him to shut up, but he doesn't listen. Surprise, surprise.

Right now, Ike's sitting at his station, chewing on a gingerbread cookie. He has a box in front of him, one of those gingerbread house kits you buy at the store.

"Expecting a quiet night?" I ask him.

He shrugs. "No one has made one yet, so why not?"

I've never understood those things. You make them. They sit there for the whole month, and then you just throw them out because if you try to eat the thing, you'll break your teeth. Yet, every year, I go to my mom's, and we have a contest on who can make the wackiest gingerbread house. It makes her happy, and that's what counts.

I leave Ike to his fun and head to Milo Brandt's room. His chart comes with an old newspaper photo of a kid in a too-big smock, paint on his hands, holding up a wooden top. The caption calls him *a toymaker's legacy.* Now, he's thirty-six and has throat cancer. The oncology nurse warned me that his voice cuts out when he pushes it.

"You're early," I tell him. "I'll be honest. Didn't expect to see you up here so soon."

His voice is rough and low. "Sorry to disappoint," he says. He looks past me to check the doorway, the wreath, the hall. "Deal still good?"

"You going to give me what I asked for?"

We had a chat once a few years ago that left me intrigued with his story.

He gives one slow nod.

"Then the deal is still good."

The heater kicks on and off. No rhythm.

"Where do you want me to start?" he asks.

"Start where everyone thinks they know you," I say.

The corner of his mouth pulls up. "That would be the shop," he says.

CHAPTER 2
MILO

The shop smelled like wood, glue, and old varnish. My father spent more time there than at home. He said wood made sense. It didn't argue if you knew what you were doing.

He taught me to sand before he let me carve. "The finish is what people touch," he said. "It's the part they remember."

He handed me a block that was roughly shaped and told me to make it ready for a child. I worked until the edges stopped scratching my skin.

Parents brought their kids in on weekends with their mittens on strings, their boots dragging snow. The parents all used my father's first name. They would tell him what birthday was coming and what grade the kid was in. He would remember the kids the next year without checking a book.

He was basically the village Santa Clause, if you think about it.

He fixed other people's toys for free—broken wheels, missing buttons, cracked bodies. "If it breaks, bring it home," he'd say, and people did.

I swept the floor, emptied bins, and wiped counters. People called me *the helper*. They thought I'd just become him one day. No one checked if that was what I wanted.

I learned patterns. I would place a toy in a kid's hands so they looked at me for a second instead of him. I would to give them something slightly off so they'd come back and I'd see them again —a stiff wheel or a loose screw that wouldn't fall out but would squeak over time. Nothing dangerous, but it was enough for me to feel like I mattered.

You can call that cruel if you want, and it was. It was also the only way I knew I was there. The town only saw my father, so I had to arrange faults if I wanted a piece of that attention.

CHAPTER 3
MILO TO JACK

Have you ever worked with wood? Did you ever think of being a carpenter when you were a kid, building things? All it takes is being able to understand the tools around you, but not everyone can do it.

I want to make one thing clear before I say anything else. I'm not here trying to find forgiveness. Not from you. Not from the big guy upstairs. It's not that I don't think I need it or deserve it. I just don't care for it. Sharing my story, telling the truth... it's about being real. Some people mistake that for confessing, but you don't, do you?

All I want is to be able to tell my story the way I want to tell it, not the way people want to hear it. Does that make sense?

CHAPTER 4
MILO

I was twelve when I made the hiding game.

It started because it rained for weeks. Parents were tired, and kids wound up. The shop filled up. My father couldn't watch all of them and work at the same time, so I made up a game.

I told the younger kids we were on a ship. The floor was water, and the counters were islands. The toy chests were safe spots when the storm hit. I turned our kitchen timer and called out, "Storm," and they all ran to hide. At first, I hid with them, so they'd play. Then I stopped. Someone had to keep count. I liked standing in the middle and knowing where everyone was.

There was one chest by the window that got the afternoon light. It was a simple box, hinged lid, padded inside. A boy named Theo liked it. He was small and quiet until he laughed. When he laughed, adults relaxed. That kind of kid.

He'd climb in, pull the lid down to a crack, and wait for me to call time. He always went back there. I told him the same rule every time. "Leave a gap so you can breathe." I showed him with my hand, two fingers' worth of space. I believed that meant he'd be safe.

On the day everything went wrong, there was a real storm

outside. Wind, heavy rain, the works. The shop was busier than usual. Parents wanted somewhere dry and predictable.

I started the game, set the timer, and said, "Storm." The kids hid—one behind the counter, one under a rack, and a couple in the back room. Theo went to his chest.

While they were hiding, a girl came in crying. Her kite had torn. Her mother was angry, not at her but at the wasted money. My father stepped in and promised he could fix it. I watched him and thought if I could fix it first, maybe she'd look at me instead.

The timer went off. I called time. Kids came out laughing and shouting. All but Theo.

I called his name. Once. Twice. The third time, my father turned. I knew he knew something was wrong. By then, the chest had gone silent.

We opened the completely shut chest. No gap. He was inside, not breathing. We pulled him out. Someone ran for the clinic. Someone shouted for an ambulance. Someone said, "Accident."

It was an accident, but it was also the result of a game I had built, a rule I had set, and a moment I hadn't watched. That part is mine.

CHAPTER 5
JACK

There's a pause that shows up when someone finally names the thing they've been avoiding. Machines keep going, and lights hum, but everything feels like it's waiting to see if the speaker will keep going or shut down.

Milo's voice scrapes out after talking about the chest. He coughs hard enough to make the monitor chirp and then level out again. He looks at me like he's daring me to change the subject.

I don't say sorry. That word doesn't fix anything in here.

I turn his cup so the handle is in reach again. "Drink," I say. "Then we'll keep going."

He takes a small sip. I can see that it hurts him.

"Ready?" I ask.

"Next part," he says with a nod.

CHAPTER 6
MILO

When a child dies in a small town, everyone decides who they want to be. Fast.

They called it a tragedy. That word lets people keep living the same way with less guilt. They cooked casseroles and offered their prayers. They filled the church for the funeral. They told my father they were praying for him. They told me to "stay strong for your dad."

My father closed the shop for a week. When he opened again, his hair was shorter. That was the only visible change. He told me the game was over. No more hiding.

He put more unfinished toys on my bench. "Work," he said. "We make it better now."

Theo's mother came by once. She stopped in the doorway and stared at my father. She didn't step inside. They spoke quietly, too low for me to hear, but the sound of her breathing cut through everything. When she left, she forgot one of Theo's blue, small mittens on the counter. My father picked it up and put it in the drawer with his tape measure. He never moved it again.

The chest got turned into a table. Dad took the lid off and put catalogs on top. No one spoke about why. No one removed it from the shop. That was his solution—hide the thing in plain sight and pretend that was enough.

People needed the store to stay what it had been, a place where broken things got fixed, so they forgave my father. They kept bringing in toys and broken things and stories about their kids. They went right back to "If it breaks, bring it home."

I kept introducing small flaws so that things would keep coming back. I left a wheel just slightly off. I left a joint that would get loose over time. Nothing that would hurt anyone. Just enough that the toy would return and I'd matter for ten minutes.

I never touched a chest again. I didn't have to. That part of the damage was already done.

Instead, I started testing things.

Not people. Not yet. Objects first. Small ones.

I'd rub a wheel too tight into its groove to see how long it took before the strain showed. I'd sand one side more than the other so a toy leaned when it stood. I'd carve a hinge with three clean notches and one that didn't line up. That's where the truth lived—in the one wrong line.

Customers brought things back the way parishioners bring sins to an altar. "My daughter says the doll won't close its eyes anymore." "The horse leg won't stay straight." "The music box has a hiccup."

My father apologized even when he wasn't at fault. He'd take the toy back, turn it over, and start talking to it like an injured pet.

He never looked at me.

The town started bringing more repairs than sales. They wanted him to fix everything, and he wanted to give them that.

I wanted to see how much they'd tolerate before they noticed me.

When a child cries because a toy doesn't behave, the room holds its breath. You learn what people value by what they rush to fix first.

If a wheel broke too soon, they blamed the manufacturer. If it broke much later, they blamed themselves. I learned to aim for the middle, the moment where doubt tastes like guilt.

One mother asked if her son had damaged the toy by accident. I could feel the lie forming in the room before anyone said it.

I said nothing.

My father apologized again. The mother nodded, and the boy cried.

I watched the boy's face and realized something important—a toymaker can hurt a child without ever touching them.

I didn't want to be forgiven anymore. I wanted to be noticed.

The second child wasn't supposed to get hurt. Not physically at least. That wasn't the point.

Her name was Mara Lynn. She was six years old with a soft voice. She liked the wooden birds my father made and always asked for ones "with brave colors."

I watched her choose one, hold it up to the light, and ask my father if birds slept with their eyes open. He answered her like she was asking something sacred.

She never looked at me, so I made a test for her.

Not the chest. Never again. A different kind of test.

I set a row of tops on the counter where she always stood. Nine tops spun straight. One top had a flaw in the center post, small but fatal. It wobbled fast but unpredictable.

I watched her choose.

She picked the flawed one. I was surprised. She spun it. It shuddered, scraped, and fell. Confused, she frowned and tried again. Her mother told her to "use gentle hands." She did.

It failed again.

Her chin trembled, and she whispered, "I broke it."

The mother scolded her for not respecting nice things.

My father stepped in, apologized again, and replaced the top with one of the flawless ones.

She spun it. Perfect.

Her mother said, "See? That's how good toys behave."

The girl nodded, but something in her expression had changed. She didn't look at toys—or at herself—the same way. She left the shop quieter and smaller.

That's when I understood the power in the smallest wrongness.

I didn't need to hurt bodies. I could hurt certainty. I could move a child's sense of self off its foundation with nothing more than a carved mistake.

I tested the town that winter. Not often and not violently. Just enough to see who trusted themselves and who trusted the toy.

My father called it a hard winter for repairs, but I called it learning.

CHAPTER 7
MILO TO JACK

People think the fire was the first violent act. It wasn't. It was the first visible one.

By the time I lit the match, the shop had already burned through everything that had made it honest.

The town didn't blame me for Theo. They blamed the hinge. They blamed the chest. They blamed the idea of accident.

They needed the shop to stay magical. They needed my father to stay pure. They needed me to stay invisible.

You can only scrub yourself out of a story for so long before your hands start shaking.

The week before Christmas, three families brought toys back. Every one of them was one of mine, flawed by design.

My father didn't ask questions. He just fixed them. He always fixed things.

He never asked why I was breaking them.

I don't think he wanted the truth. He wanted the shop and what it represented.

Every Christmas Eve, the town had a traditional caroling walk. They would start at the bakery, go to the church steps, and then head to the old hotel and other places. We were the final stop, the "heart" of the route according to the flyers.

The night the carolers came, I realized something simple. As long as the shop existed, he would forgive me faster than I could breathe. He would make the town forgive me too. He would sand my sins down into a story that made sense to them.

I wasn't ready to be forgiven.

So I removed the setting. If a man becomes a place and you want the man back, you take the place away.

I didn't plan for the fire to spread that quickly. I didn't plan for the beams to catch. I planned for destruction, not danger.

That's the part no one believes.

My father ran inside. Of course he did. The shop was the part of himself he understood.

He came out coughing and empty-handed. He looked at me. He wasn't scared. He was disappointed.

That look was the first honest thing he'd given me in years.

He never forgave me for that one.

Good. I didn't want the kind of love that made no demands.

CHAPTER 8
MILO

We kept the shop open eight more Christmas seasons after Theo. Kids and their parents still came. The town let the story fade because it made life easier.

I got older and grew taller than my father. He worked more slowly and talked less, but he still took every broken thing that came through the door, and he still fixed them without taking money if the family couldn't pay. The town loved him for it. The articles in the local paper never mentioned me.

Remember the Christmas tradition with the town? The caroling walk came to our shop, and my father opened the door wide. The crowd sang. Kids waved at the window display. He talked about one more year of traditions.

I stood in the back room and looked at the piles of toys waiting for repair. Some were mine, but some weren't. I looked at the chest-turned-table with the catalogs on it. I opened the tape-measure drawer and saw the blue mitten still there, exactly where he'd left it.

I was angry at the shop. Angry at the town. Angry that my father had been allowed to go on as the hero of the place while the worst thing that had happened there stayed quiet under a stack of paper.

I set the fire.

I told myself I was freeing my father from being chained to that room and freeing myself from being his shadow. I told myself that if the shop was gone, we could both stop living inside that one moment with the chest.

None of that is an excuse. It's just what I thought at the time.

When the first alarm sounded, I was already outside in the side alley. I watched the smoke build through the window, and I heard people shouting. My father ran in once and came out coughing and empty-handed. The flames were too fast for him.

He stood next to me while the fire department did what they could. He kept saying words like "wiring" and "faulty," as if explanation could change the result. No one questioned him too hard. They liked believing it was the building and not the people.

I didn't correct him. Not then and not ever.

Until now.

CHAPTER 9
MILO TO JACK

I disappointed my father a lot. I once overheard him telling someone I had issues.

Sure, I had issues. I liked to destroy things. That's what landed me in prison. That story isn't interesting. Prison itself isn't interesting. It's routine—lines and counts, noise at the wrong times and silence at the wrong times. Men compare sentences and scars. They build pecking orders out of useless details.

My father visited once, did you know that? He did everything by the book, his hands on the glass and the phone to his ear as he asked me why.

I looked at him and knew right away he wasn't asking why I did the things that landed me in trouble. He didn't want to know why I'd hurt the people I'd hurt or if I knew that people would have gotten hurt when I destroyed the things I did.

He wanted to know why I burned down the shop.

He wouldn't have been able to handle the real answer. I already knew that. His heart wasn't good. It was like I broke him as I slowly broke myself.

I told him I was angry and stupid and said I knew he needed the money from the insurance. That wasn't true, but it was the kind of lie people understand.

He nodded, but he knew I'd lied.

We sat there in that stale visiting room and pretended we had said enough. He never came again. He sent catalogs instead. Old habit.

When the doctors told me about the cancer in my throat. They used long words, but I heard only one thing—you're going to lose the main tool you used to dodge the truth. Talking, yelling, avoiding... all gone.

Here's what I haven't told anyone else, Jack. I know exactly when my voice started to fail. It was the first time I would have called my father to confess and didn't. The phone was in my hand, but I put it down. My throat has been closing ever since.

I never understood why I'd been transferred from that prison to here. I'm not crazy, I just did crazy things even in prison. Finally, I wasn't being overlooked. People saw me, and I liked that. This place, though... I lost all of that. I became a thing. I became invisible. That's the goal of a place like this, isn't it? To make things forgettable?

So instead of doing crazy shit like I would before, I guess I became my father. I became known for fixing things—the tray wheels, the laundry cart, the loose screw on the door hinge... It wasn't kindness. It was... Well, I guess it was habit. I started becoming the person I never wanted to be, and by doing that, I was noticed.

CHAPTER 10
MILO

After my father stopped visiting, I wrote a letter. I told him I forgave him for carrying the town's forgiveness alone. I told him I forgave him for never saying my name in public when Theo's came up. I told him I forgave him for believing the fire story he preferred.

None of that was true. I wanted him to be angry. At me. At the shop. At himself. Anger would have meant we still had something between us. Instead, he sent silence and mail-order catalogs.

I ended the letter with *your son who finally understands you.* I stared at that line for an hour then burned the paper in the metal trash can by the laundry. It was one honest action in the whole exercise.

I spent my life fixing things so people wouldn't have to look at me. When I finally made something that couldn't be repaired, they had no choice. I forced them to see the worst version of me. I'm not proud of that, but I won't pretend it belongs to anyone else.

And now I'm here in your bed, on your floor, tied in, and I realize I've come full circle, haven't I? To wanting my father's attention to becoming him. Would he be proud? Probably not. I hurt too many people along the way. Killed too many too.

CHAPTER 11
JACK

He dies at 2:13 a.m.

Milo didn't get into the dirty, which surprised me. Before coming here, he'd killed a total of twelve people. Mostly by setting people on fire with gasoline. Turns out, Milo had a thing for fire.

I do the work—check the pupils, confirm no pulse, straighten the sheet, and remove the restraints. Basic respect.

Ike steps into the doorway, sees the body, and nods once. No jokes. He backs out and closes the door halfway. That's our version of a sign on the handle.

Some patients break without warning. Some break on purpose. Milo falls in the second group. My job isn't to glue him back together. It's to remember it was his choice.

The donation bin is full. I drop another gift card on top and push the lid down.

Then I sit down and help Ike finish his stupid gingerbread house.

NIGHT 6: CASSANDRA

CASSANDRA INTRO

Day shift added more decorations. Ike adjusts every single one and then night shift adds our own.

Tonight's patient is **Cassandra Holt**, fifty-two, former foster-care caseworker. Quiet. Keeps her hands folded like she's waiting to be called in for a meeting she already knows the outcome of.

The chart says she "misfiled" children. That's the sanitized version. The real story is she built a private system inside the public one. Her own set of rules about who deserved safety and who didn't. People called it a sorting error. She called it efficiency.

She asked for me.

Said she didn't want to die "misunderstood."

That's usually code for: *someone finally needs to hear this the way I meant it.*

She keeps tapping her thumbnail against the rail. Left-right-left. A habit she used to use to keep track of kids who didn't come back when they were supposed to. Habits tell the truth even when the mouth doesn't.

Night Six.

Let's see what she's ready to admit.

CHAPTER 1
JACK

There's an unspoken rule in the Death Ward—December confessions don't wait to be asked for. They hunt you down.

Maybe it's the lights someone keeps hanging where they don't belong, or maybe it's just the season making everyone feel like their ghosts deserve a holiday too. Either way, I barely have time to sit before another miracle that shouldn't exist finds its way to me. And this one? She doesn't bother knocking.

Cassandra Myles arrives just after shift change. She has close-cropped hair and is in hospital grays. Her wrists are marked from IVs and older scars.

When I head into her room, her eyes are closed. I'm not sure if she's sleeping or resting. To pass the time, I look at her file—former child protection caseworker, multiple suicide attempts, "possible homicide admissions" not pursued in court. From what I heard, she had been transferred here as a means of saving her life.

Child killers don't tend to do well in general prisons. Here, she's just another inmate hidden away so everyone forgets her.

Cassandra has been on my list for a while. It's not because of what she did. More about why. People like her, especially women like her, I don't understand. I'm not judging. I'm just curious.

When I look up, her eyes are open, and she's watching me.

"You took your time," she says. Her voice is thin and steady.

"I could say the same about you."

She smiles. "Still a smart ass, aren't you?"

"You don't look too good, Cassandra."

I'm not lying. She's aged over the years. She's now seventy-three, but she looks close to ninety.

She rolls her eyes. "Does anyone when they're on your floor?"

Good point.

"Ready to talk? Or do you want a little bit? I just brewed a fresh pot of coffee since I heard you might be in the mood for a chat." I wait by the end of her bed. Regardless of what she says, I'm getting my coffee.

"Go get your coffee. Add some whiskey too. You're going to need it." She coughs.

I bring her cup up to her lips and let her take a few sips. Her throat catches, and I know it's painful for her to swallow. I don't rush her.

Hospice taught me patience. The Death Ward reinforces that lesson daily.

CHAPTER 2
CASSANDRA

I started out as reception for the CPSD. Child Protection and Support Division. It was an easy entry-level job—phones, forms, directions to the bathroom… that kind of thing. When angry or scared parents walked through the door, they needed a calming presence to meet them. When the kids came in quiet or loud, they needed to know they were safe.

It didn't take me long to learn what was needed and expected. The person who trained me, she had a calmness about her that I tried to emulate. She had a way of telling a person to take a seat without it coming across as rude, and people listened. They would even said thank you.

My goal was to move up, and as soon as there was an opening, I put my name in. I went from reception to intakes, and let me tell you, that took some getting used to. Home visits, case notes… The job is simple on paper—keep kids safe. In practice, it means you drive, you write, and you argue with budgets. You tell yourself you are a wall between children and whatever wants to hurt them.

For the first few years, I believed that. I thought if we worked faster, if we followed protocol, if we cared harder, we could stop the worst of it. Then, the first boy on my caseload killed a neighbor's cat, and everyone called it "acting out." Six years later, I saw his name in a news article about an assault. Different city. Same face. Nobody was surprised.

We had no system for that. We had forms for bruises but not for the look some kids get when you say "no" and they look at you like you're a problem to solve. We had checkboxes for substance use, truancy, and hunger but nothing for the way a child watches other people hurt and tests how much they enjoy it.

I sat in too many meetings where we called patterns "risk factors" and moved on because the marks weren't bad enough yet. I watched kids we all worried about turn into adults we all pretended not to know. After a while, it felt dishonest. We said we believed in prevention, but all our tools were built for cleanup.

I'm sure things are different now.

At the time, there was nothing in place for kids like that, so I started keeping my own notes.

The first page wasn't much. Just the names of the ones who unsettled me more than the others. Not the loud ones who slammed doors or the desperate ones who lied about everything because the truth was too heavy. No, these were different. They didn't cry or rage. They studied. They watched you the entire time you wrote your notes. They smiled when you told them something wasn't allowed. They took quiet pleasure in small cruelties, things adults brushed off as "kids being kids." At first, I told myself the list was just a personal aid, something to help me keep track of the cases that needed extra attention, but it grew. A few names became ten then fifteen. Some aged out and moved on, but others stayed in the system long enough for me to notice the same glint behind their eyes in every stage of childhood.

That glint never softened with therapy or a change with new foster homes. That glint wasn't caused by trauma. Sometimes, it came from kids who had loving parents, stable homes, and opportunities. That was what frightened me most.

You can explain away pain. You can explain away fear. You cannot explain away pleasure.

The pleasure of watching someone else suffer.

That wasn't in any of the manuals I was given to read.

I didn't show the list to anyone. It felt like admitting I was seeing things I shouldn't be able to see or things I wasn't supposed to name. Our field is built on hope. You don't get to look at a child and say, "This one won't stop." You're supposed to believe they can. You're supposed to believe there's a treatment plan, a school program, a mentorship, or a placement that will steer them back before it's too late.

But I watched too many slip past the point where help meant anything.

Sometimes, the parents saw it too. They would sit across from me, wringing their hands while their child waited in the hallway. They would whisper things. "He scares his sister." "She stands over me at night." "I don't know why, but I'm afraid of my own child." I would nod and write down the words we were trained to use. "Challenging behaviors." "Parental anxiety." "Family stress." Those sanitized phrases made everyone feel like we were still in control.

But we weren't.

Not with those kids.

The beginning of the second list came after a home visit in winter. An eight-year-old girl met me at the door with a smile that didn't reach her eyes. The house smelled like cinnamon—her mother had been baking—and everything looked normal. Too normal. Like a display of what a safe home should be.

The girl followed me room to room without being asked. She didn't speak. She just watched me with open curiosity like I was the one being evaluated. When I bent to check her younger brother's toys, she whispered something behind me. It had been too soft to catch, but the tone chilled me. Her mother brushed it off as "a phase."

Three months later, the girl cornered a child at school and held her there until a teacher intervened. No marks. No injuries. Nothing you could write up as anything other than "peer conflict." But the teacher's face when she described it? That told the story.

That girl became the first entry on what I came to call the Checklist.

It wasn't formal. Just observations. Three markers that, when all present, suggested a child wasn't just troubled. They were testing limits most children never consider.

I didn't show the checklist to anyone. They wouldn't have understood. Or worse, they would have dismissed it as my imagination.

But once I created it, I couldn't stop seeing it. One name after another.

Sometimes a child met only one marker. Sometimes two. I watched those children closely. Sometimes they grew out of it. Age softened them, environment shaped them, or interventions actually worked.

But for the ones who met all three? The ones who watched me like the girl from the winter house had? They stayed on the list.

The problem with seeing patterns is that once you recognize them, it becomes impossible to ignore what they imply.

No one prepares you for the moment you look at a child and understand that they don't need protection. They need boundaries the system refuses to enforce.

Everyone wants the narrative of the hurt child, the saved child, the redeemed child. No one wants to talk about the ones who find harm interesting.

So I kept my notes. My list. My checklist.

The more I wrote, the more it felt like I was finally naming the thing nobody else dared to. Not because I wanted to be right. God, no. I wanted to be wrong. I wanted someone to tell me I was misreading everything, that these kids would be fine, that I was seeing shadows in daylight.

But then the files started piling up. Public ones. Articles. Juvenile reports. Transfers to facilities in other states. I recognized the names.

Two from my list were involved in group assaults.

One disappeared from our caseload after "running away," and months later, I found her referenced in a report about a fire.

One became the subject of a late-night news segment. Nothing graphic, nothing explicit, just the kind of story that makes viewers lock their doors halfway through.

I read each piece with the same sick certainty that even if I had spoken up, nothing would have changed.

It felt like watching a wave form miles from shore. You knew exactly where it would break, but you were told your job wasn't to warn anyone. No, your job was to stand there and measure the water afterwards.

That's when I realized the system wasn't built to stop what was coming, so I would have to build something myself.

I didn't decide it all at once. It wasn't a revelation or a vow. It was a slow understanding, like the gradual darkening of a room when the sun sets and nobody turns on a light.

Prevention wasn't possible, but intervention? That was different.

So I kept my notes. I expanded them. I created a structure. A checklist. A truth the department didn't want but desperately needed.

Eventually, I began to act on it.

CHAPTER 3
CASSANDRA TO JACK

I didn't call it a checklist at first. It was merely reminders in the margin, a red dot in the corner of a file, a word underlined twice. Then I noticed the same three things showing up in the kids who scared me in a way bruises didn't.

First was the enjoyment of harm. Not anger. Not self-defense. Enjoyment. The child who smiles after pushing another down the stairs. The one who relaxes when an animal flinches. They look more at the reaction than the injury.

Second was a lack of attachment. Not shyness. Not trauma numbness. A blankness when you ask who would you miss? The answer, no one, is delivered without drama. They don't bargain for people. They bargain for objects, privileges, and exits.

Third was rehearsal. Small tests. They start fires in bins behind the school and watch. They take more risks close to adults just to clock who intervenes and how. It isn't impulsive. It's practice.

One of these on its own, I noted. Two together, I worried. All three... Every case I'd ever had with all three turned into something worse by adulthood. Not always criminal, sometimes just destructive in quieter ways. But harm followed them.

The file words for this are "conduct disorder," "oppositional," or "possible emerging personality traits." These words don't move resources, though. They sit there while the child grows older and stronger. Then we act surprised when the outcome matches the pattern we ignored.

I put the three items on a page in my own notebook. Three lines. I told myself it was for focus. I wanted to know where to put more support, where to push for placements, where to ask for residential programs that never have space.

But it became more than that.

CHAPTER 4
JACK

I've heard a lot of ways people justify harm. "It was an accident." "I lost control." "I snapped." Cassandra hasn't used any of those. She lays out data, three points in a row. No emotion, no apology, just the kind of clarity that tells me she's been rehearsing this long before she ever ended up on my floor.

Most patients try to convince me. Cassandra explains.

"What did you do when a kid hit all three?" I ask.

Her eyes flick. Not at me. Past my shoulder toward the half-closed door. The hallway hums with the usual nighttime static—a rolling cart, a distant cough, the building settling. Whatever she's remembering exists outside all of that.

She breathes in long and slow, like she's bracing herself before stepping into cold water. "That's the part nobody wrote down," she says.

Her voice doesn't shake. That's the detail that gets me. People tremble when they're lying. They falter when they're excusing themselves. When they've already made peace with what they've done, they sound like this—steady and resigned.

"Tell me. I'll write it," I tell her.

She studies me for a full beat. Assessing. Weighing.She nods once, the movement small but certain.

Outside her room, someone drags a chair across the floor. Cassandra doesn't flinch. It's like the ward has disappeared for her. It's just the two of us and the truth she's finally ready to lift into the light.

She leans forward slightly. "Then listen carefully," she says.

CHAPTER 5
CASSANDRA

The first one was a girl. Twelve. I won't give you her name. You don't need it. She had a younger brother. He was afraid of her in a way he couldn't explain.

She enjoyed causing harm. I saw it when she described fights at school. Her eyes would be flat when she talked about her own bruises, but they would brighten when she described the others. No remorse. Only interest.

She had no attachments. When I asked who she trusted, she shrugged. When I asked who she would call if she was in trouble, she asked why she would do that.

"People make things worse," she said. "I fix my own problems."

She rehearsed with small fires and small lies, testing whether adults believed her or her brother. She kept a list of what worked. She didn't hide that from me. She assumed a social worker would appreciate the research.

We tried services, counseling, in-school support, and mentoring. She treated them as more practice. Her brother kept getting hurt. Nothing that would get her removed, though. Scratches, sprains, one concussion that could be explained away because he "slipped" on ice.

I knew where this was going. I had a stack of old files that showed me the path—police reports later, hospital charts, a future partner with broken teeth. Maybe a child would sit across from some other worker and say, "I'm afraid of her," and not be believed.

I requested a different placement. It was denied. Not enough proof. I requested respite for the brother. That was denied. No funding. I wrote that I believed serious harm was likely. My supervisor changed "likely" to "possible" in the system. That's how the agency stays afloat. Words are soften until danger looks manageable.

I sat with three checkmarks in my notebook for a month. During that time, she broke the family cat's leg and lied about it. Her brother lied too, but his lies were defensive. He lied to cover for her because it was safer than telling the truth.

That happens a lot.

When the family called to report her missing, I already knew what I was going to do. I guided the mother through the "runaway" script and told the police exactly what to write. I emphasized the conflicts at home, and I mentioned boys she had talked about. Cheap distractions.

I knew where she was. I had been the last adult she saw who wasn't afraid of her.

CHAPTER 6
CASSANDRA TO JACK

The rest, I will not spell out for you. You don't need the details. All you need to know is that when they called her a runaway and closed the file, I felt relief instead of panic.

Her brother stopped flinching. His grades went up. He slept. He grew into someone who might not hurt other people for sport.

One disappearance meant one family was out of the blast radius.

In my mind, that was prevention.

In case I'm not being clear enough, I made sure that girl wouldn't hurt another person. I knew no one else would stop her until it was too late.

So I did what no one else would or could do.

And yes, if you need specifics, I killed her. It wasn't hard. She actually came up with the idea. I think it was a test to see how far I would go. She said she'd heard that you can knock someone out by having them breath something in. She said she should probably test it to see if it's true.

She meant to test it on me. She had the washcloth in a bag, and I could smell it as soon as she opened it up. She calmly walked up me, but she didn't expect me to grab her hand and force her to knock herself out with the cloth.

After that, I realized I needed to get rid of her.

They never found her body. They found a few of the others but didn't tie them to me. Not right away. When they're listed as runaways, finding them in dumpsters or abandoned sheds and buildings doesn't really scream they were killed, you know.

And yes, if you need to put a label on it, serial murderer would count. I wouldn't have said that way back when, but I've had a lot of time to think about what I did.

Who would have thought little old me would be a serial killer? Back then, I was just handling a problem everyone else wanted to ignore.

CHAPTER 7
CASSANDRA

One child meeting the checklist looks like a crisis. More than one is a pattern. Over ten years, I saw the same pattern again and again. Different faces, different files. Same eyes when harm happened. Same lack of ties. Same practice runs.

The system called them "chronic behavior concerns." Schools suspended them. Parents begged for help and were told to wait. Therapists wrote long notes about trauma and attachment and the need for more time.

Time is what these kids used to get better at what they were already doing.

So, I started a ledger. Not in the agency database. In a note-book I kept at home.

First name, age, three boxes. When the boxes were all checked, I marked the date and track of every "intervention" we had tried. I wanted to be sure I wasn't reacting out of frustration. I wanted evidence that the system had nothing else to offer.

There were twelve names in that ledger. Twelve kids I believe would have gone on to hurt others badly.

Maybe some would think that's arrogance. I think it's experience.

I kept seeing the same movie, and I got tired of pretending the ending was a surprise.

Each one disappeared. Each one recorded as a runaway. Different circumstances. Different methods.

I made sure there were enough details to satisfy the forms but nothing that would keep the case open for long. I did not involve anyone else. No partners. No witnesses as far as I knew.

I kept the ledger with my checklist because I wanted to see what I was doing.

Was I a hero? No, I never saw myself like that. I saw myself as a filter. The world keeps producing people who enjoy harm. The least I could do, I thought, was limit the number.

CHAPTER 8
CASSANDRA TO JACK

I knew exactly what I was doing. Don't get me wrong.

I chose each step. I tested nothing on impulse. That's the point, right? Impulse is how people excuse themselves.

I'm only here because someone found my ledger and was scared. Not of me or what I did. No, they saw the mountain of problems that would come their way and so they decided to hide me away while they fixed the problem behind the scenes.

I honestly never thought I'd get found out. I never thought it would be someone so close to me who would tell on me.

CHAPTER 9
CASSANDRA

I kept the ledger under a false bottom in my bedroom closet. It was a simple hiding place. I wasn't worried. Nobody visits a social worker's house unless they have to. We spend all our time in other people's living rooms.

I slipped. Not with the killing. With my own health. Long hours, bad food, no time off. One day, my chest hurt, and my left arm went numb. I ended up in the ER. It was a panic attack, not a heart attack, but they kept me overnight.

My sister came by to bring clothes. She decided to clean. She's always been like that. She rearranged my drawers, sorted my laundry, and found the ledger.

She read enough to understand what it was. She took it to a pastor she trusted, who took it to a council member who owed him a favor.

That man took it to a deputy director at my department.

By the time I was discharged, there were three missed calls from my supervisor and a message asking me to come in for "a discussion about concerns."

The tone was careful. I heard that tone in pre-removal meetings. It means we know enough to be angry and scared but not enough to decide who else is at fault.

I understood that if the ledger moved further up, it would not stop with me. It would pull in every manager who had changed "likely" to "possible." Every administrator who had denied a placement. Every politician who had voted down funding and then posed for photographs with "at-risk youth."

They did not care about the children I killed. If they had, they would have cared about them when they had been still alive.

They cared about the potential scandal. Headlines about a "Child Protection Serial Killer" are bad for budgets but are even worse for careers.

I went home and took enough pills to make my body stop. I thought I wouldn't wake up.

Unfortunately, I did.

The deputy director visited me in the hospital. He talked about mental health. He said they all missed the signs. He wanted it to be about me and not the kids. Not them and their problems and their avoidance. I was too dangerous to be tried in public.

Rather than put up a fight, I went with it. I was tired, and I knew what court would look like—years of hearings, dozens of people pretending they never saw what they saw, and children paraded as proof we did some good. I did not want to give them that show.

They never told me where they were sending me, but they said I would be safer in a secure facility. What they meant was that the department would be safer if I disappeared.

Basically, I became a runaway as far as everyone was concerned. I disappeared, and as far as I know, no one has looked for me.

CHAPTER 10
CASSANDRA TO JACK

You asked for the part I haven't given them. Fine. Here it is.

I regret that I believed I could tell the difference between a damaged child and a dangerous one with certainty. I regret that I did not fight harder for more options before I decided there were none. I regret that I used the word "runaway" for kids who never got to choose where their feet went.

I don't regret protecting the siblings, the classmates. I've seen what people with those three traits do when they grow up and the world keeps failing to stop them. I sleep more now here than I did when I was chasing files that never closed.

If you want me to say I am sorry to the twelve, I can say the words, but they will not be honest. I am sorry that the world built them and then handed them to me with no tools outside of paper and time. I am sorry that I believed I was the only one who saw the pattern. Lone savior thinking is a professional hazard.

The truth is simple. I built a checklist and a ledger because I was tired of watching harm play out in slow motion. I stepped in and chose a line nobody gave me permission to draw. That is what they should write down. Not "monster." Not "angel." Just "worker who refused to follow instructions."

CHAPTER 11
JACK

She is quieter after that. Her eyes stay on the window, looking out at the thin dusting of snow.

"What do you want me to do with this?" I don't know why I'm asking because it really doesn't matter in the end.

"Whatever you want," she says.

I check her vitals. The numbers are not good. Her lungs are tired, and her heart is working harder than it should.

"Do you think I'm wrong?" she asks.

"I think you're dangerous," I say, "and I think you spent twenty years watching other dangerous people get away with it."

"That's not an answer," she says.

"It's the only one I've got," I tell her. "This floor doesn't do easy answers."

She closes her eyes. "That's fair."

Later, when the ward falls into that long shallow hour before morning and her breathing slips, I sit with her. No monitor alarm. No drama. Just a body that has done too much deciding finally running out of decisions.

I didn't need to do anything on my part. Her body decided it was done. She fell asleep on her own, and then her heart stopped.

Some runaways make it back. Some are pushed. Some are erased. My job isn't to sort them. My job is to remember who they were when they decided to be honest.

NIGHT 7: GIDEON

GIDEON INTRO

The vents rattle like they're arguing with themselves. They do that when the temperature drops too fast. December gives this place edges.

Tonight's patient is **Gideon Vale**, sixty-one. Retired security guard that worked in a mall. The nurses say he startles at footsteps but not alarms. That tells you who he was listening for.

The police wrote "overreaction."

The papers wrote "mall tragedy."

His file says "loss of boundary judgment."

That's all shorthand for: *he picked the wrong moment to protect the wrong person.*

He hasn't spoken since arrival.

But he nods when I enter.

There's recognition there — not of me, but of the job. He spent his life watching doors. Men like that need someone to stand in one with them at the end.

Night Seven.

Time to get the version that never made it past the food court.

CHAPTER 1
JACK

The vents rattle like they're arguing with themselves. They do that when the temperature drops too quickly. December gives this place edges. Everything sharpens—the cold, the quiet. Even the way patients look at me when they've run out of road.

Tonight's patient is Gideon Vale. He's sixty-one, a retired mall security guard. He mostly worked nights. He's the kind of man everyone forgets about until the alarm goes off or the lights flicker.

The nurses say he startles at footsteps but not alarms. That tells you exactly who he was listening for.

The police wrote, "Overreaction." The papers printed, "Mall tragedy." His file says, "Loss of boundary judgment."

In other words, he picked the wrong moment to protect the wrong person.

He hasn't spoken since he came to the asylum. Not a word, not a whisper. I don't know if he can't or just hasn't. There is a difference.

When I step into his room, he nods. There's recognition in that gesture, not of me but of the job. We're both men who've spent our lives watching doors. The difference is I open mine when the worst finally walks through.

Men like Gideon always carry the same expression at the end —a mix of exhaustion and ritual, like they're still waiting for one last shift to start. They've built their whole identity around standing guard, and they don't know how to put the position down.

He doesn't look fragile. He looks... unfinished. There's still something in him held rigid, something he hasn't unclenched since the day everything went sideways under fluorescent lights and Christmas decorations.

I sit. He watches. The vents rattle overhead. Somewhere down the hall, a patient laughs.

"Do you think it's time?" I ask. "Time to give me the version that never made it past the food court."

He blinks once slow and deliberate, and then he smiles as my words register. Finally, his throat works like it's remembering how to form words and starts swallowing.

I let him take a long pull from the straw and wait to see if he needs more water before he begins.

CHAPTER 2
GIDEON TO JACK

You ever notice how people only hear alarms when they're meant for them?

In the mall, we tested the fire system every month. Full drills. Sirens, lights, and a prerecorded voice telling everyone to proceed to the nearest exit. Half the time, people kept eating, kept shopping. Until someone starts shouting, everyone figures it's a test, or a glitch, or somebody else's problem. You can blast a warning through every speaker there is and still, nothing.

But one kid crying? That cuts through everything even when it's not there.

The first time I heard it, I thought it was a real child. Why wouldn't I? That's my job, right? Keep an eye out. Notice who's alone, who's scared, who's... wrong.

And I did notice. I noticed every damn time. That's the problem.

I'll tell you how it started, and you can decide if I ever had a chance of stopping.

The first time I heard the child, I was alone on night shift. I followed the sound into a hallway no one else believed in.

CHAPTER 3
GIDEON

I had been working security at the mall for almost fifteen years when I heard the first cry.

It was a Thursday in November, late enough in the evening that the air outside had dropped below freezing but early enough inside that the speakers were still playing regular pop instead of holiday music. The mall was between seasons. It was after Halloween but not quite Thanksgiving, and there certainly wasn't any Santa or lights being hung.

I liked that time of year. The crowds thinned out during the weekdays, and the people who did come in had purpose. They were in and out. No loitering teenagers trying to ride the escalators backward, no groups of kids daring each other to sneak into the service corridors. That night, it was just workers closing up their shops, older couples finishing up their walking laps, and a few parents with strollers heading toward the exits.

I made this round the way I always did—a slow circuit past the anchor stores, a sweep through the food court, a glance at the restrooms, and a nod to the janitor buffing the tiles to a shine. Nothing out of the ordinary. Nothing that should have lodged in my memory.

But when I turned into the short staff hallway between the shoe store and the discount clothing place, I heard it.

A child crying.

Not a tantrum. Not the high, sharp whine of a kid who'd been told no. This was smaller, closer to a sob, the kind children make when they're trying not to make noise at all.

I stopped and listened.

"Hello?" I called out. "Anybody back here?"

The sound came again, soft and choked, like it was being swallowed by the walls.

I followed it.

The service corridor wasn't long. It bent once at a dull angle past a door marked MAINTENANCE ONLY. The fluorescent light overhead flickered, and the buzzing got into my teeth. The crying seemed to echo ahead of me, always just around the corner, always just one step farther than I was.

"Hey," I tried again, gentler. "You lost? You hurt?"

No answer. Just that wet, muffled sound.

I reached the end of the hallway. A dead end. A locked door leading to the back lot. No branching paths. No janitor's closet. No utility room, not here. I knew the floor plan. I walked it every night.

The crying stopped.

I stood there, staring at the door, my hand hovering over the key at my belt as if a child might simply appear if I turned the knob. The glass inset in the door showed only the empty employee parking lot lit by a single sodium lamp that made everything the color of an old bruise.

I checked the corners and the ceiling. I even checked my radio just in case something had come over the line that my brain had turned into a cry.

Nothing.

On my way back to the main corridor, I passed the MAINTE-NANCE ONLY door and listened. Silence.

By the time I reached the food court, I half convinced myself it had been a sound from outside warped by the vent systems—a fox, a cat, or a baby in a nearby apartment. Buildings carried noises weirdly. You could never entirely trust where something came from.

Still, that night, when I sat in front of the monitors, I pulled up the feeds for every camera covering that stretch of the mall. I watched the timestamp roll through the minute I'd entered the service hall. Nobody else was there.

I rewound and watched it again.

The next morning, I told myself I'd imagined it. Long shifts, poor sleep, the hum of the lights… any of that could make anyone hear things.

I didn't mention it in the log, but a week later, it happened again.

Holiday decorations had gone up overnight—garlands strung along the railings, enormous ornaments suspended from the ceiling, and cardboard presents clustered on fake snow. The music had shifted, bells in every song.

I was midway through my circuit when the crying started again.

Same sound. Same quality. A small, desperate child holding their breath between each broken breath.

Only this time, it wasn't coming from an empty service corridor. It seemed to drift out from the crowd itself.

I stopped at the top of the escalator, scanning below. Parents with bags. Kids dragging behind. Two teenagers in matching hoodies. A group of middle schoolers locked to their phones.

I focused on the nearest potential source—a boy, maybe eight, standing too close to the edge of the fountain. His mother barked at him to step back. He complied, his face sullen but dry. No, not him.

The cry came again. It was impossibly close, like someone whispering directly into my ear.

I turned. A young man in a dark jacket was moving quickly

along the upper level. He wasn't quite running, not quite walking. His eyes were fixed straight ahead, his shoulders hunched. No kids. No bags. His hands empty.

I moved to follow him. "Sir? Excuse me, sir!"

The man didn't slow.

I quickened my pace, cutting through a cluster of shoppers. The crying layered over the mall's music, the bells inside the speakers jangling in time with the child's hitched breaths.

"Sir!" I reached out, my fingers catching the man's elbow.

The man jerked away like he'd been shocked. "What the hell?" he snapped, turning on me with wide, startled eyes. "Don't touch me."

I looked around, expecting—hoping—to see a child nearby. There was no one within arm's reach except a middle-aged woman with a shopping bag and a bored teenager leaning against the railing.

"Where is the child?" I asked, scanning the floor, the benches, the spaces between. "You hear that?"

"Hear what?" the man demanded. His face was flushed now. "You can't just grab people—"

"Sir, I heard—"

"Call your manager," the man said, pointing a rigid finger toward my chest. "Call them right now. I'm filing a complaint."

The crying stopped as abruptly as it had begun, and the silence that followed made me dizzy.

My supervisor was called. The man gave her an angry, detailed statement about being accosted by an overzealous guard. I tried to explain that I heard something, that I thought a child was in distress, that I was acting out of caution.

My supervisor's eyes slid past me toward the crowd, toward the stores, toward the bottom line.

"It's the holidays, Gideon," she said quietly after the man stormed off. "You can't just go putting hands on people because you hear something. You understand?"

I understood.

That night, I watched the cameras again. No crying on the audio feed. No child in the footage.

The next day, the complaint form appeared in my personnel file, tucked behind a write-up for "inappropriate physical contact" and "unverified concern."

I signed where they told me to, pen digging into the paper.

CHAPTER 4
GIDEON TO JACK

It should've stopped there. I know that. First time, maybe it's the building. Second time, maybe it's stress. You tell yourself to let it go and pretend you didn't hear it after all.

But I know I did.

My coworkers said it could have been something in the ductwork or the heating system. Maybe it was just the mall settling like buildings like to do. Doesn't matter what it was. I heard it.

They sent me to a counselor after the second complaint. They called it employee wellness. The therapist asked if I'd ever lost a child. They all ask that. My answer is always no. Not sure anyone ever believes, me though.

The real answer? Between you and me, I didn't have one to lose, and that was more of a problem, don't you think?

Then she asked if I had nightmares. Who doesn't?

She suggested I take a few days off to rest.

Like rest could fix it.

The sound, the cry, it followed me home.

I'd be sitting my chair TV on low. I'd close my eyes, and there it would be. Not from the set. From the walls. It was always just past where I could get to. Always sounded the same, like a little kid trying not to cry too loudly but you knew they were scared.

I still hear it, you know. Different vents and different walls but the same cry.

Can I ask a favor? Can you check the hallway for me? Just once. Just to confirm there's nothing there.

While you do that, I'll tell you about the night with the Christmas tree, considering it's the holidays and all.

CHAPTER 5
GIDEON

By the time December rolled into full swing, I had three complaints in my file.

Each one followed the same pattern. I heard the crying, identified a person the sound seemed to cling to, intervened, and was punished for overstepping. No children were ever found. No missing persons reported. No crimes recorded. Just a guard "escalating" situations that management deemed routine.

"We're not the police," my supervisor reminded me after the third incident. "We're here to observe, report, and de-escalate. You can't go chasing ghosts."

Except, I wasn't chasing ghosts.

I was docked a week's pay and reduced hours. They framed it as a chance for me to "reset."

But the sound didn't care about schedules.

It called to me in grocery store aisles, between the clink of glass jars and the squeak of carts. It threaded through the static of my television late at night. It slipped between songs on the radio while I sat in traffic, caught at red lights that lasted too long.

It was always the same—soft, contained, and desperate, a child's attempt to cry as quietly as possible.

I started sleeping with the TV on, not for company but for cover.

The mall unveiled its Christmas centerpiece in the central atrium two weeks before the holiday—a forty-foot artificial tree strung with tens of thousands of lights. Santa's village sprouted beneath it, complete with a throne, a line of red velvet ropes, and a photographer charging twenty dollars a print.

The first weekend, the place was packed with kids in holiday sweaters, parents juggling strollers and coffee, and teenagers taking selfies under the fake snow. Music blared from hidden speakers, the same four songs on loop.

I was assigned to crowd management. Stay visible, my supervisor told me. Smile. Help with directions. Keep the line moving.

I stood near the base of the tree, close enough to see the reflection of all that motion in the mirrored ornaments. The air smelled like cinnamon pretzels and body odour.

For the first hour, the noise crowded out everything else. Children wailed when they were told they had to wait. Babies shrieked when placed on Santa's lap. The photographer snapped, cooed, and herded families along.

I watched it all with detached focus. I scanned faces, hands, and movements. No one lingered near the edges longer than they should. No one circled the line twice. I could almost believe, for that one suspended slice of time, that the crying had been nothing more than a misfiring memory.

Then, between one flash of the camera and the next, the sound cut through the chaos.

A crying child.

Not the angry scream of a kid denied a candy cane. Not the bored whine of someone done with waiting. That same small, strangled sob, thin as a thread and twice as sharp.

It didn't come from the line. It didn't come from Santa's throne.

It wove out from the back of the scene, from behind the false storefronts and cardboard cutouts that made up the village façade, where a narrow staff corridor led toward the service hallways.

My head snapped toward it, but no one else reacted.

"Do you hear that?" I asked the nearby elf, a teenager in a polyester costume and a bored expression.

"Hear what?" she asked, not looking at me.

The sound came again, louder, as if the child had given up on being quiet.

I stepped away from the line.

"Hey," the elf said, "we need you on this side. People keep trying to cut."

"I'll be right back," I told her. My heart pounded in my throat. "Call Mark if there's trouble."

I left and followed the cry.

Behind the wooden storefronts, the festive veneer dropped away. There was exposed framework, power cords snaking along the floor, and a stack of extra decorations waiting to be rotated in.

The staff door stood slightly ajar, a wedge of dim hallway visible beyond.

The crying came from deeper inside.

"Hello? Security here." I called out. "Is someone back there?"

No answer. Just the echo of my own voice… and the crying ahead.

I pushed the door open and stepped through.

The light in the service corridor was weaker than in the public area. One of the overhead fixtures was out, leaving a soft shadow near the middle section. The walls were scuffed, bearing the marks of years of equipment being wheeled through.

At the far end, a figure in a dark jacket walked away from me, shoulders hunched, pace brisk.

My gaze snagged on the tilt of the person's head. They weren't turned toward the exit. They were angled slightly toward the wall, as if leaning close to… someone. Something.

The cry cut off mid-breath, and the figure stiffened.

The hallway wasn't long. My boots thudded on the concrete as I closed the distance.

"Turn around," I ordered. "Now."

The person half turned, enough for me to see the flash of a middle-aged man's face. He looked harried, startled, and more annoyed than frightened.

"What's your problem?" the man demanded. "I got turned—"

"Where's the child?"

"What child?"

"The one crying. I heard them. They were right here."

"There's nobody here but you and me," the man snapped. "You've got the whole mall out there. Go guard that."

Every nerve lit up, I looked past him. The corridor was empty. No doors. No alcoves. Nowhere a child could have gone in the seconds since he'd stepped inside.

My skin prickled. "Move away from the wall," I said.

The man threw up his hands. "You know what? I'm going to management. This harassment needs to stop. I've heard about you."

He brushed my shoulder as he pushed past me and stormed toward the door. I nearly reached out to stop him, but the echoes of the previous complaints tugged my arm back.

My radio crackled. "Gideon, status?" my supervisor's voice snapped. "Line's backing up out here."

"On my way," I said, staring down the empty corridor one last time.

I returned to the tree. The elf gave me a stink eye. The line had doubled. Santa looked sweaty. Nobody seemed panicked. No child appeared as noticeably distressed as the cry I heard.

CHAPTER 6
GIDEON

The night of the tragedy, the mall was open late. Christmas Eve extended hours. A shift where time got gummy and lost its edges.

I was back at the tree.

They'd warned me after the last incident that I couldn't leave my assigned post unless directed. No more "interventions" based on noises no one else heard. I nodded, promised, and signed another form. I needed the job. The job needed me to be predictable.

The crying started just after nine.

The sound hit me so hard my vision fuzzed for a second. A child was sobbing in terror, gulping air between each broken plea. It came from everywhere and nowhere, weaving through the music, the chatter, and the announcements over the PA.

My hand clenched the small radio clipped to my vest. "Do you hear that?"

The elf shook her head, eyes on the crowd. "Hear what?"

The cry rose, not in volume but in intensity. The verbal shape of it stayed indistinct, but the emotion… that was unmistakable.

Help.

This time, when I turned, I didn't see a corridor or a lonely figure in a jacket. I saw a man at the edge of the crowd standing stock-still. He was in his early thirties, clean-cut, and wore a dark coat and jeans. No bags. No kids nearby. His hands were tucked into his pockets, his shoulders tight.

I moved before I knew what I was doing. "Sir," I called, stepping away from the tree.

"Gideon," the elf said sharply. "We talked about this. Stay here."

I ignored her. The crying threaded between my ribs.

"Sir!" I called again.

The man turned, his eyes jerking toward me like he'd been caught doing something he shouldn't. His mouth opened then snapped shut. He pivoted and started walking toward the side exit that led to the quieter wing of the mall.

"Sir, I need you to stop," I said, weaving through the crowd.

A woman with a stroller swore as I passed too close. An older man startled, his hand flying to his chest.

The crying grew more frantic. It didn't sound like it was coming from the man, or from the air, or from anywhere logical at all.

It sounded like it was lodged inside my skull.

"Security!" someone called behind me. "Where's security going?"

I reached the man near the base of the escalator. "Stop," I said, my hand extended. I wasn't touching him yet. "I just want to ask you a question."

The man half turned, backing away. His foot planted unsteadily on the first step of the moving escalator.

"What is wrong with you?" he snapped loud enough that heads turned. The escalator kept pulling him backward. "I haven't done anything—"

"Where is the child?" I was trying not to yell, but my voice cracked. "I hear them. I've been hearing them—"

"There is no child!" the man shouted.

The words hit me like a slap.

No child.

No child in the hallway. No child in the corridor. No child on the footage.

No child.

The escalator carried the man upward toward the second level. He twisted to look back at me, anger bleeding into fear as I caught sight of the people now staring, phones raised, whispering.

The crying keened inside my head. My vision tightened. The edges of the world blurred and faded, everything narrowing down to the moving metal steps and the man balanced wrong.

"Sir, step off," I said, suddenly aware of the danger. "You're going to—"

The man's heel slipped.

It didn't take much. A sudden jerk. A startled flail for the handrail. The crowd's collective intake of breath. A body tipping backward into the people behind him, feet tangling with the steps, a chain reaction of limbs and momentum.

Someone screamed. This voice was older than a child's, strangled with shock.

The escalator kept moving.

I lunged forward, grabbing for the emergency stop, but in the seconds it took to fight through the onlookers, the damage was done. Bodies jostled. A woman fell. A child clung to the rail, his eyes huge. A man hit the metal with a sickening sound that would replay itself in my mind for the rest of my life.

The escalator ground to a halt under my hand.

Silence.

Then chaos.

People shouted and called for help. Phones dialed emergency numbers. Management rushed over. Santa stood halfway out of his throne, his hat askew.

I didn't hear a child's cry now. Just adult voices full of blame and fear.

When the paramedics arrived, they took three people out on stretchers.

One of them died.

The footage aired on the local news that night over and over. Grainy security video of a guard pursuing a man toward the escalator, of a confrontation that seemed to spring from nowhere, of a fall that could be paused and replayed until every frame was an indictment.

The anchor spoke in sober tones about holiday tragedy, about a "security overreaction," about the need for better training. Witnesses were interviewed. Some said the guard had been agitated. Some said he'd been shouting about a child nobody saw.

The mall issued a statement. So did the police.

No missing children were reported that night. No lost little coats. No distraught parents. No unanswered calls to customer service.

In the small hours before dawn, after the questioning and the forms and the suspension, I sat alone in the break room, staring at my hands.

The crying came from the vending machine this time, from somewhere behind the metal coils and blinking lights.

I pressed my palms over my ears, but it made no difference at all.

CHAPTER 7
GIDEON TO JACK

They put reckless this, negligent that on the papers. Some people wanted worse and said I should be locked up forever. Others said it was a tragic mistake.

That word again. Tragic. Like a story with a nice arc.

But it wasn't a mistake, not to me, and it wasn't random. It was the end of something that had been following me for years. It was the moment everybody else finally saw the mess that had been in my head the whole time.

The counselor brought up hearing tests, auditory processing, trauma. She asked if I'd ever been around an accident when I was younger, something with a child involved.

When I was eleven, my mother had taken me to a shopping center. It was smaller than the mall I ended up working in, rougher too. Back then, nobody talked about predators and safety plans, not the way they do now. She parked me on a bench while she went into a store and told me to stay put.

There was a little girl crying across from me. She was maybe five. No adult in sight. Every time someone walked past, she would stiffen up and go quiet. Then, she would start again once they were gone.

I didn't do anything. I sat there and listened. I watched adults walk by and pretend not to see. I told myself it wasn't my business, that her parents would come back soon, that if she really needed help, someone older would step in. No one ever did, though.

I don't know what happened to her. Maybe nothing. Maybe her mom came back with an armload of groceries, and everyone went home just fine. But that sound—her trying not to sob loud enough to attract the wrong kind of attention—stuck with me.

That's the voice I heard years later over and over.

So when you ask if I lost a child, the answer is no, but I abandoned one, and that's worse. You can't lose what you never bothered to hold onto.

Can you check the hallway again? Please?

CHAPTER 8
JACK

The corridor outside Gideon's room is the same as every other on the Death Ward—pale walls, polished floor, and doors that all look identical until you know the people behind them.

I've spent enough nights here to know how sound works in this place. You can hear a scream from three rooms over and nothing at all from the bed next to you. It all depends on where it hits the angles.

I stop under the junction where two ducts meet.

If I really want to, I could make something of the thin hiss of air or the occasional creak. I could say it sounds like a breath caught at the top of a sob or like the swallowed tail of a cry.

But that's the problem with working in a place like this. If you listen long enough, the building will give you whatever you're already afraid of.

I close my eyes anyway. "Nothing," I tell myself.

The vents answer with a shudder.

I open my eyes and go back into Gideon's room.

His gaze hooks onto me the second I cross the threshold. "Well?" he asks.

I set the chart back in its holder. "Nothing out there."

CHAPTER 9
GIDEON

After the escalator incident, I didn't go back to the mall.

At first, I was suspended pending investigation. The charges were discussed, debated, and adjusted. Lawyers weighed intent and outcome. Some wanted to make an example of me. Others argued I'd already been punished enough.

In the end, the compromise was a mixture of accountability and diagnosis.

Reckless endangerment. Involuntary manslaughter. Questions about my mental state at the time. Evaluations that underlined my hypervigilance, my auditory hallucinations, and my obsession with one particular pattern of sound.

I was moved from holding cells to hospital wards to, eventually, places like this one.

At every stop along the way, the crying followed.

It wasn't constant. It would come in pulses. Weeks would pass in sterile quiet. Days were divided into group sessions and medication times, the nights into the long, flat stretches of institutional dark. Then, a new building would shudder in cold weather, or a plumbing system would groan, or an old duct would whistle, and the sound would thread its way back into my ears.

Child. Small. Trying not to be heard.

I reported it once, early on, to a psychiatric nurse during an intake. It was reported as auditory hallucinations.

I never mentioned it again.

I learned to keep my eyes on the visible crises—the man pacing the ward muttering about invisible wires, the woman who refused to sit unless all the chairs were facing north, and the young inmate who flinched at every footstep and begged anyone who passed his door to check that the locks still worked.

Compared to them, I felt almost ordinary.

Except for the sound.

At night, lying on whichever institutional mattress I'd been assigned, I would stare at the ceiling and inventory the options.

Either the crying was real and I was the only person in a series of buildings consistently willing to respond... or the crying was not real and I'd built my life around chasing it anyway.

Both possibilities condemned me.

CHAPTER 10
JACK

Gideon's voice frays at the edges by the time he finishes. Not from volume. He's never raised it once. From the effort of hauling every piece of that story into the open.

"So," he says, staring at the ceiling, "are you sure you heard nothing out there?"

He asks it like a man bracing for his sentence.

I lean back in the chair. The vents rattle overhead, same as before. Same argument with the weather. Same breath of the building.

"I heard an old asylum on a cold night," I say. "Vents, pipes. The usual."

His jaw tightens. "Nothing else?"

"That's all I can swear to," I tell him.

His eyes flick to mine, searching for something—pity, maybe, or confirmation that I'm lying to make him feel better. I don't give him either.

"I'm not saying you didn't hear what you heard," I add. "I'm saying I didn't. That's all."

He exhales a broken half-laugh. "Then it's still just me," he says.

"In here?" I tap my temple. "Maybe. Out there?" I nod toward the hall. "You're not the only one who's ever chased something nobody else could see."

He studies me. "You hear anything?" he asks. "Ever?"

I think of all the years on this floor. Of the way the building stores voices and leaks them at odd hours. Of the times I've sworn I heard a name whispered from an empty room or a laugh from a patient long dead. Of the line between the living and the dying and how thin it gets in December.

"Sometimes," I admit. "I don't go running after it."

"Maybe that's where I went wrong," Gideon says.

"Maybe," I say, "or maybe you went wrong when you remained sitting on that bench."

His eyes widen. For a second, the guard drops, and there's the eleven-year-old boy under all the uniforms and years.

"Thought you'd missed that part," he says.

"I don't miss much," I tell him. "Occupational hazard."

Silence settles between us. Not empty. Just resting.

"You want the deal?" I ask him at last. "The real one. No cameras. No letters. Just you, me, and whatever's left of the night."

He swallows. "What's the deal?"

"Since you told me the version that didn't make it past the food court, the one nobody wanted to put on the news, I'll tell you this—you're not on duty anymore, Gideon. There are no doors left for you to guard and no alarms left for you to chase. If that sound comes again, you don't have to follow it."

"That's not how it works," he whispers.

"Maybe not," I say, "but you've never tried not responding. Might be worth a test."

His gaze drifts back up to the vent. "What if it's real this time?" he asks.

"Then someone else will get there for once," I say.

His fingers loosen on the rail, one by one, until his hand falls open on the blanket.

On my way out, the vents above the door give one last shudder. If I listen too hard, I can almost shape it into a small, choked sound. A child, maybe.

Or just the building complaining about the cold.

I don't turn back.

NIGHT 8: CASSIAN

CASSIAN INTRO

The day shift brought in hot cocoa in one of those ancient crockpots that should've been retired with the last hospital renovation we never got.

Ike decided to "improve it" with peppermint schnapps.

So now the whole Death Ward smells like someone tried to host a Christmas party inside a prison cell.

Festive, if you don't think too hard about it.

Tonight's patient is **Cassian Holt**, thirty-two.

You won't find much noise in his file. Men like him don't make noise—they remove it. Quiet walker, steady gaze, like he's always checking the exits even when he's sitting still.

During intake, he refused to touch the chair. Not out of attitude—out of reflex, like he'd learned once that chairs were for people who didn't need to be ready.

When I asked why he was transferred up here to the Death Ward, he gave me a line that didn't settle right until the Warden confirmed it.

"I don't keep trophies," Cassian said. "I keep records."

Nobody says that with innocence.

He requested tonight.

Volunteered.

Confessions like that come from people who've been holding something too heavy for too long.

Night Eight.

Cassian Holt.

Let's see what kind of truth he thinks needs to be told before Christmas.

CHAPTER 1
JACK

The chapel is the only room in this place that still pretends to be comforting. Someone put up a plastic wreath over the door, and there's a nativity set on the back shelf. Half the figures are chipped. The stained glass doesn't show much anymore, but nobody comes to the chapel for the scenery.

People come for the bell.

You can't see the bell from the pews. It hangs in a cramped loft above the ceiling. The nurses say it hasn't been part of any official procedure in decades. Not for fire drills. Not for announcements.

I can't believe they even have it to be honest. It's not like it's used every Sunday or anything.

In fact, it only rings when Brother Cassian decides it should.

Tonight's patient is Cassian. He's in his fifties, an ex-monk turned full-time preacher, convinced he's doing God's book-keeping.

The last time I saw him, he asked if I wanted to confess. I told him he didn't have enough time left in the my shift.

Now, it's his turn.

He's not on the ward tonight, though. Considering it's the end, they brought him down to the chapel instead of keeping him in his room. Maybe someone thought the chapel would keep him calm.

Let me make one thing clear—Cassian is not an inmate. He started off as staff and somehow ended up being a houseguest who settled into a room and never left.

Cassian sits in the front pew like he's waiting for a service to start. His hands are folded in his lap. His eyes are steady. He looks at the rope like it's the only thing in the room worth noticing.

"If you ring a bell long enough," I say, "even God stops listening."

He lifts his head at that. Recognition. Approval, maybe.

"This is new for me," I admit.

He smirks. "Now you're in my playground. Listening to confessions is a natural element to the chapel, don't you think? Seems kind of fitting, even though I didn't ask for it."

I watch him, searching his face and his posture, and then check the equipment by his side. He's not looking good, and to be honest, I don't imagine we'll be down here long.

"This is where I want to go, Jack. Here. Not in a bed upstairs."

"You might not be able to make deals with God, but you can with me. You know that."

He nods. "I remember our deal. A story for a lasting sleep. Are you ready?"

CHAPTER 2
CASSIAN

I entered the monastery when I was nineteen. I wasn't drawn by faith the way the others were. I just wanted quiet, the kind that didn't shift every few minutes, the kind that came naturally.

The monastery gave me that quiet. Stone corridors, slow footsteps, the same prayers repeated until they turned into background noise… It was orderly in a way the outside world never could be.

The bell tower was where I ended up spending most of my free time, not because they asked me to but because the sound made sense to me. One action, one result. You pulled. It answered. No guessing. No hidden motives.

The older monk in charge of ringing showed me the rhythm. He told me to let the bell carry its own weight. I learned how to time each strike so the sound didn't blur.

I know I wanted quiet and ended up ringing the bell, which is the opposite of quiet, I was in control of the noise instead of the noise controlling the chaos around me.

The death toll was different from everything else—three sets of three and then one strike for each decade of the brother's life. When a man was near the end, the infirmarian let the tower know. The bell marked the moment for everyone living around us.

People paused their meals. Doors opened, and prayers began. The sound spread farther than anything spoken inside those walls. For a few minutes, a dying man wasn't leaving the world alone.

The first time I helped ring for a death, I understood why the ritual mattered. The bell filled the courtyard and kept going. It didn't stop at the walls. It carried up the hill and across the fields. It reached anyone who cared enough to listen. It felt like I was doing something practical in a situation where you couldn't do much at all.

The trouble started the night the bell didn't ring.

One of the older brothers died in his sleep. They found him at morning prayer. He was already cold. Nobody had been with him. Nobody had known he was close to death. There was no signal to the tower, no tolling, nothing to acknowledge the moment he left his body. We buried him the same as the others, but the silence around his death stayed with me.

After that, I started watching the older men more closely. I paid attention to changes in their routines, who struggled during work and who seemed winded during chapel. I told myself I was being careful. What I really felt was the need to make sure the bell never missed again.

I began ringing at times when I wasn't assigned—short tolls late at night when I thought someone was declining. I kept the rope steady so it wouldn't make enough noise to wake the whole monastery. I just wanted the bell to reach whoever needed it.

A novice admitted he was doubting his vocation, and I rang for him too. A villager died unexpectedly after his time had already been marked, and I rang again. I thought every strike had purpose. Looking back, I know I was searching for reasons to pull that rope.

The leadership noticed. They told me the tower wasn't mine to use. They said the bell had meaning only when it followed the rules set for it. They warned me to leave the tolling to those assigned to it.

I agreed, but the urge didn't go anywhere.

I avoided the tower for weeks, but every time someone limped, coughed, or looked pale after evening prayer, I thought of that silent death and the brother who had been buried without a single note to send him off.

I lasted a month before I started again. Quietly, carefully, just enough to feel like the world wasn't turning without someone keeping track of who was about to fall.

Over time, the bell felt less like a tool and more like the only language I trusted. People lied. People hid. People kept their fear tucked away. The bell didn't do any of that. It said what needed to be said. It didn't wait.

When I left the monastery, the sound came with me. Not the real bell. The need to strike something into the air when a soul was close to slipping.

I thought leaving would cure it, but it didn't. It only followed me into the next place that was willing to hand me a key.

CHAPTER 3
CASSIAN TO JACK

How many jobs have you held over the years? Do you remember what it was like leaving them? Maybe you were forced to, or maybe it was your choice, but there's always a sense of ending, right?

Sometimes you change how you live, how you react, how you think, mainly because leaving gives you the opportunity to start something new... or maybe to become someone new.

Me, when I left the monastery, I felt lost. I had no idea what to do or who to be. The brothers told me I needed rest and guidance, but they really meant was that I needed to get out before I became a problem they couldn't manage.

So I left and tried to live quietly. I worked small jobs, rented a small room over the hardware store, and went to Mass every Sunday.

But the need to hear the bell never left me.

You don't understand. That's okay. Not many do.

Every place I went, I listened for the bell. I would hear a cough in a grocery store or a cough from across the street, and something in me would tighten the same way it used to when the infirmarian came looking for the tower keys. I kept telling myself it was habit, but it wasn't. It was need.

Have you ever had a need like that?

200

It takes over. It's full and complete, and it's all you can focus on. It was all I focused on, that's for sure.

CHAPTER 4
CASSIAN

After a while, I knew I had to find a place where people passed in and out the way they did at the monastery. Somewhere with routine. Somewhere with endings. I looked for hospitals and community centers, anywhere that needed a chaplain or a caretaker. This place had an opening in the chapel. I walked in, and they accepted me without much fuss.

The first week I was here, a patient died in the early hours. No bell. No announcement. No sign that anything had shifted. Staff came in, recorded the time, and moved on. The silence felt exactly like the night that old brother slipped away without a single toll.

So I rang the bell—three sets of three. Just enough to mark the moment. Just enough so the world might feel it for a breath or two.

They warned me the next morning and told me the bell wasn't part of the protocol and that patients didn't need something like that echoing through the walls at night.

I ignored it. A bell that never rings is just decoration. If it exists, it should mean something.

And once I started again, I couldn't stop.

Not because I wanted attention, or power, or control. I couldn't stop because every time the air in this place changed, I felt the same urgency I used to feel in the tower. Someone was slipping. Someone needed marking. Someone needed the world to know they were gone.

That worked for a while. I rang for the dying then for the ones who were close then for the ones who were lost in other ways. When I started running out of reasons, I made more.

By then, I wasn't ringing for who was dying. I was ringing for who needed saving.

Even if they didn't think they did.

When I took over the chapel, the bell was already half-forgotten. It hung in the loft above the ceiling with no list, no schedule, no task attached to it. Most staff didn't know the rope still worked. They assumed the whole thing was ornamental, another leftover from when this place tried to look gentler than it was.

For the first few months, I rang only when someone was close to the end. I listened the same way I used to listen in the monastery. You learn the signs after a while—breathing that falls out of rhythm, a kind of stillness in the body that isn't sleep, rooms that feel emptied out even before the monitor gives up. I marked those moments with short tolls. Nothing dramatic. Just a signal that someone had reached their final hours.

I told myself that was all I would ever do.

But then I started noticing other things—a man in withdrawal who begged for a chance to tell the truth and then swallowed it when a nurse walked in, a woman who hadn't slept in four days because she was convinced her dead sister stood at the foot of her bed, a young inmate who spent every night pacing in circles because he was certain he heard footsteps behind him. None of them were dying, but all of them were close to despair, fear, or hopelessness. It didn't feel right to wait for their bodies to give out before marking the moment.

The bell had always been used to warn, not just mourn, so I rang for them too—short tolls at steady intervals.

I thought I was doing something helpful, something that

acknowledged they were struggling in ways the rest of the world preferred not to see.

Once I widened the definition, it kept widening.

There were staff members who moved through the ward with a kind of practiced indifference—a technician who snapped at patients when he thought nobody heard, a nurse who used her keys like a weapon of authority, a counselor who lied to a man about his treatment plan just to get him to cooperate. I told myself they needed marking as well. Not as a punishment but as a reminder. The bell had corrected me once. Maybe it could correct them.

I started ringing more often. Twice a week. Then three times. Midnight became the hour that made the most sense. The quietest. The clearest. If the bell was going to carry any meaning at all, it had to cut through a time when nobody could pretend they didn't hear it.

The complaints began after the sixth week.

Patients said the sound woke them and left them terrified. Staff said they couldn't tell if it meant an emergency. Administration told me the bell created "unnecessary agitation."

They used the same words the abbot used years earlier. They didn't understand what I was trying to prevent.

By then, I had already convinced myself that every toll meant the difference between a soul being noticed or overlooked. It didn't matter that the people around me disagreed. I believed I knew what was at stake.

That belief became a kind of momentum. Once it started, it didn't slow down.

I rang for the man who refused to eat, convinced his food was poisoned.

I rang for a woman who apologized to everyone she met as though she were preparing for a final judgment.

I rang for a man who told me he had no one outside these walls and no one inside them either. He said the world would be better if he disappeared.

I rang the bell twice that night, once when he said it and once after he fell asleep.

I didn't see it as obsession. I saw it as duty.

Eventually, I reached a point where almost everyone seemed at risk of slipping in one direction or another. The bell became a way of keeping track, of reminding myself that someone's pain mattered, of giving a weight to the moments that would otherwise go unnoticed.

The problem was that I didn't have enough moments left to mark.

So I began creating them.

I told a man in detox that his roommate resented him.

I asked a woman if she was certain her children remembered her.

I whispered questions into the ears of patients who were already unsure of themselves. Nothing violent. Nothing physical. Just enough doubt to draw out confessions they refused to give willingly.

Once the fear surfaced, the bell followed.

In my mind, the two things became linked—cause and effect, tension and release.

I knew it was slipping out of control. I knew the line I had drawn around what qualified as a warning was expanding too fast. But by then, I was convinced that if I stopped, everyone I had marked would fall into the same silence as that old brother decades before.

By Christmas Eve, I had rung the bell more times in three months than the monastery had rung it in five years, and the meaning I had assigned to each toll was no longer something anyone else could recognize.

I thought I was saving people.

I didn't realize how many I was pushing to the edge.

CHAPTER 5
CASSIAN TO JACK

I know what you're wondering. You want to know when I realized I'd gone too far. You want to know if there was a moment where I stopped and said, "This isn't what the bell is for."

I wish I could give you that moment. It would make the rest of what I'm about to tell you easier for both of us.

The truth is, it didn't feel wrong when I was doing it. It felt necessary.

You've walked these halls long enough to know how quickly people disappear without leaving the building. Not physically. I mean the way they sink into themselves, the way they stop making eye contact, and the way they give up on the idea that anyone would notice if they slipped.

I thought the bell could break through that. I thought a sound that strong might pull someone back before they went too far.

When they told me I had to stop, I didn't hear correction. I heard fear. I thought they were afraid of what the bell revealed more than the bell itself. I thought they didn't want to acknowledge how close so many people were to falling.

You've seen the files. You know how many patients here are running from something that already swallowed them. I convinced myself I was the only one willing to say it out loud.

And then I ran out of reasons to ring.

That was the part I wasn't prepared for — the stillness, the waiting, the sense that I had let the rope rest long enough for something to slip past me.

I started paying attention to smaller things — a nurse raising her voice, a staff member skipping a step in a routine, a patient telling a half-truth instead of a whole one.

None of it meant anything on its own, but I treated each moment like the start of something larger. I told myself that if I didn't mark it now, I'd regret it later.

They unhooked the bell after I rang during a night shift meeting. They disconnected the rope completely and wrapped it around itself so no one could reach it. They thought that would solve everything.

But it didn't stop anything. It only made the sound louder in my head.

I kept ringing it anyway. Not with my hands. With the memory. With the pattern. Three sets of three then the age and then whatever felt necessary after that. I told patients the bell was still tolling for them. Some believed me because they wanted the world to acknowledge their suffering. Others believed me because they feared what the toll meant.

That's when things began to fracture. Not just in them. In me.

I can see your question already. Why didn't I stop? The answer is simple. I thought I was the only person willing to carry the burden. I thought everyone else was pretending.

And once you believe that, stopping feels like letting the entire floor fall at once.

You want the rest? Fine. You can have it. Just understand that by Christmas Eve, I wasn't ringing for the dying, or the afraid, or the hopeless.

I was ringing because silence had started to feel like abandonment, and I couldn't bear that again.

CHAPTER 6
CASSIAN

Christmas Eve was always difficult in this place. Too much expectation in the air. Too many memories hovering over people who didn't have the strength to carry them.

The staff tried their best. They put up decorations, played quiet music, and handed out cards with generic messages inside them, but it only made the emptiness sharper.

I had been ringing the bell internally for weeks by then. I still felt the pattern in my chest. I counted the beats without realizing it. I woke up at midnight even on nights when nothing was wrong. I couldn't tell where the habit ended and the compulsion began.

On the night before Christmas, I walked the chapel before any of the staff arrived. The tree someone had put up leaned slightly to one side. The lights flickered. There was a small table covered with cards patients had written. Most of them were unsigned.

When I stood under the loft, I felt the same weight I used to feel in the monastery tower. There was a shift in the air, a sort of pressure that told me someone was slipping again.

It didn't matter that no one had died that day. It didn't matter that the ward had been calm. The moment I stepped into that room, I felt an absence I couldn't name.

So I went looking for who it belonged to.

Some of the inmates had gathered in the dayroom. They were restless and tired. A few tried to hum along to the music on the television. Others kept their heads down.

One man sat alone, staring at the floor and whispering apologies to someone who wasn't there. I watched him for a long time, waiting for the moment when he would lift his head or blink or show some sign that he was still connected to the world around him.

He didn't, and that was enough for me.

I left the dayroom and went back to the chapel, convinced the bell needed to be rung even if no one else agreed. I knew the rope was disconnected, but I also knew the weight at the end of it was still real.

If I pulled hard enough, the bell might still move. Even if it didn't, the act would count. That was what I believed. The intention mattered more than the sound.

I wrapped my hands around the coil of rope they had tied back. I tried to find the rhythm I used to know—three sets of three, the years, the final toll. It lived in my memory clearer than anything else.

I pulled. Nothing happened.

I pulled again. Still nothing.

But in my mind, the bell was already ringing. I could feel the vibrations through my palms. I could hear the echo moving down through the rafters.

Someone must have heard me moving around up there because the lights in the hallway flickered, and footsteps approached the door. When I turned, a nurse stood there. She looked tired and frustrated as she asked what I thought I was doing. I didn't answer. I didn't think she would understand. I believed the bell had to answer the silence before anything worse happened.

She told me to stop. She told me I was frightening people.

She was right, but in that moment, I convinced myself she was wrong.

The confusion started because a few of the patients had seen me in the chapel and assumed something was happening.

One man began shouting that the bell was ringing for him. Another insisted it meant someone on the floor was dying. A woman started crying, saying she wasn't ready for God to take her.

The staff rushed in to calm everyone down, but fear moves faster than reason. Once it spread, it filled the entire wing.

I kept pulling at the rope even as the nurse called for help. I kept imagining the bell striking, not because I thought it would save anyone but because I couldn't face the idea of letting another night pass without marking something. Anything. I needed the world to feel it, even if it was only in a single room of a forgotten asylum.

They pulled me away before I could finish the pattern.

I remember the moment the rope slipped from my hands.

I remember the sound of people crying in the hallway.

I remember the silence after they took me down to the floor and restrained me.

That silence was worse than anything that came before it. No tolling. No recognition. No sense of weight being given to the moment. Just the empty air settling after a panic that I had caused.

That Christmas Eve was when they decided I couldn't stay in the chapel anymore. Instead of being staff, I became a patient. They moved me upstairs. They watched me closer. They stopped trusting me with anything that resembled purpose.

But the bell didn't stop for me. It kept ringing in my mind, steady and familiar.

I told myself I would stop hearing it eventually.

I was wrong.

CHAPTER 7
JACK

I've learned something about believers on this floor. They don't fold. Not the way people think. They don't break cleanly either. They bend toward whatever kept them steady the longest. Cassian bent toward bells. Some men bend toward routine, or anger, or guilt. Cassian found all of that in a rope hanging from a ceiling.

When he finishes, he sits quiet. Not waiting for forgiveness. Not waiting for judgment. Just done. Like someone who's finally reached the end of a long list.

"Is it still ringing?" I ask him.

He doesn't answer. His eyes shift toward the loft, but he doesn't move. Sometimes, silence is the closest someone like him can get to honesty.

"You don't have to mark it anymore," I tell him. "The bell. The warnings. All of it."

He exhales, slow and thin.

"That's the problem," he says. "I stopped marking things a long time ago. Now it marks me."

I don't argue. He's not wrong.

On my way out, I touch the rope. It's stiff, tied off so tightly it could be part of the wall.

Nobody's rung it since the night they dragged him upstairs. I tug, just enough to test the knot. Nothing moves. No echo. No vibration. No answering weight.

Cassian watches me from the pew. "It won't ring for you," he says. "It only rings for the ones who need saving."

"Good," I tell him. "I'm not looking for salvation."

He closes his eyes at that. Not in prayer. Just shutting down the conversation.

I step into the hallway and pull the chapel door closed behind me. The lock clicks. The vents hum. Somewhere far off, someone coughs. Ordinary sounds. Nothing that needs marking.

I don't hear anything else on my rounds that night, but once I'm halfway down the corridor, I feel the faintest vibration under my feet, and I know that is the moment Brother Cassian died.

NIGHT 9: RUTH

RUTH INTRO

Ike hung a strand of lights above the break station. One bulb keeps buzzing like it's sick of being helpful. I get it.

Tonight's patient is **Ruth Marlin**, seventy-three. Retired elementary school teacher. The type who remembers every student's middle name and never learned to retire her guilt.

The press called her the "Lunchbox Lady." I don't use nicknames. They make people smaller than what they did.

She sits with her palms flat like she's trying not to grade the room.

The restraints make her uncomfortable, but she's polite about it, which is worse.

Politeness hides more truth than anger ever could.

Night Nine.

Old sins. Long shadows. Let's hear hers on purpose.

CHAPTER 1
JACK

The blizzard started before my shift and still hasn't let up. By midnight, the courtyard is a white blur, and the parking lot looks abandoned. Half the staff didn't make it in. The ones who did came in shaking off snow and grumbling about how long it took them to get here.

Administration sends out an alert asking for anyone already on shift to stay if they can.

I offer to take the double. It isn't about being helpful. The storm makes everything too quiet, and quiet in this place never means rest.

The power flickers twice while I'm doing rounds. Long enough to make everyone tense. Generators kick in, but the lights still buzzes like they are working harder than they want to. The vents push out cold air instead of warm. Even the walls feel like they are shrinking in on themselves.

They bring in a new patient an hour after the storm peaked.

Ruth Marlin. She's seventy-three, a retired elementary school teacher. She probably kept gold stars in a drawer and never forgot a birthday.

The nurses call her polite. That's never a good sign up here.

Angry patients tell you what you're dealing with. Polite ones make you guess.

Ruth sits with her palms flat on the mattress. She's in soft restraints, and she thanks the nurse for checking them, which is worse than if she'd complained. Politeness hides things that can be dangerous.

CHAPTER 2
RUTH TO JACK

You want the truth, Jack? Fine. Everyone else has already taken their turn guessing—reporters, parents, lawyers, even former students who barely remember how to spell my name. They all thought they knew why I did what I did. None of them were even close.

I taught third grade for thirty-two years. That's long enough to see the pattern in children long before anyone else does. Who's afraid of being wrong. Who's pretending to be confident. Who's hungry. Who's lying. You can see all of it at that age if you bother to look.

Most people don't bother.

The papers called me the Lunchbox Lady because that's easier than printing what I actually did. It makes me sound silly. Harmless. Like I mixed up sandwiches.

Nobody wanted to run a headline that said the real reason. Nobody wanted to say that a teacher who spent her life taking care other people's children finally snapped when nobody listened to her.

I'm not here to defend myself. I'm not here to apologize either. You can relax. I'm too old for dramatics. But I will tell you the version nobody wanted, and you can write it in whatever notebook you're filling. Maybe someone will understand it someday.

So let's start with the children I fed.

CHAPTER 3
RUTH

Every year I taught, I kept snacks in my desk for the kids. Nothing fancy, things like crackers, raisins, granola bars, fruit cups… things that lasted. I learned early on that a hungry child doesn't think straight. They lash out, or they shut down. Nobody tests well on an empty stomach. Nobody behaves well either.

Every class had at least one child who relied on me more than the others—a boy whose mother worked too many jobs and forgot lunch twice a week, a girl who hid food in her pockets because she had two younger brothers who ate anything left on the counter, a pair of twins who shared a single lunchbox and pretended they weren't switching it back and forth.

I fed all of them. I didn't make an announcement. I didn't make it a lesson. I waited until they were busy with handwriting or art, and then I slipped something onto their desk. Most of them never said anything. They just ate quietly and moved on. That was fine with me.

The first time I noticed something was wrong with Daniel, it wasn't because he was hungry. He always had food. His lunchbox was packed neatly, labeled, organized. His mother worked at a clinic and left notes taped to the lid. He should have been the easiest child in the room.

He wasn't.

He sat stiffly, as though someone had drawn an invisible line down his spine and told him not to deviate from it. He flinched when anyone spoke too loudly. He refused help even when he didn't understand the work. He chewed each bite too slowly, like he was afraid of finishing.

The part that troubled me most was the way he watched the door. Not the clock. The door.

I asked the counselor to check on him. She nodded, wrote something in her file, and told me he was adjusting. She said children from strict homes sometimes took a while to warm up. I didn't believe her. There was a difference between strict and scared.

Over the next few weeks, Daniel began giving away pieces of his lunch—half a sandwich here, a carton of milk there. He pushed crackers toward other children even when they didn't want them. At first, I thought he was being generous. Then I realized he was watching me every time he did it, waiting to see if I'd notice.

He was trying to make his food disappear.

Children don't hide abundance. They hide struggle.

I contacted his mother. She brushed me off. She told me Daniel was dramatic, sensitive, and prone to exaggeration. She said he needed firm boundaries, not coddling. She told me to stay in my lane.

I stayed in my lane for all of twenty-four hours.

The next day, Daniel's lunchbox held only a bruised apple and a packet of crackers. The neat notes were gone. The careful packing was gone. He opened the lid and froze like he had been caught doing something wrong.

I reported it again. I documented it. I called the counselor. I called the mother a second time.

Nothing changed.

When a child starts shrinking into themselves, you can feel it before you see it. Daniel was becoming smaller every day. Not physically. Something in him was pulling inward, like he was bracing for impact that never stopped coming.

I tried to compensate. I slipped food to him during reading time. I gave him extra juice at recess. I let him help me clean up so I could talk to him without making him feel cornered. He never told me anything outright, but children communicate in other ways. He hesitated before answering every question. He apologized constantly. He watched the door more than the blackboard.

He was starving but not for food.

He was starving for safety.

When the school refused to take action, I started keeping extra records, notes about what he ate and what he didn't, how often he came to school tired and how many days he refused to take his coat off. I kept copies of everything. I even photographed his lunches when they were nearly empty.

I thought evidence would finally make someone listen.

I was wrong.

They told me I was overreacting. They told me I was too invested. They told me teachers weren't social workers and that I needed to step back before I caused trouble.

Again, I stepped back for exactly one day.

Then Daniel fainted in the hallway outside my classroom.

Every child screamed. Every adult rushed over. I already knew what had happened. Hunger wasn't the cause. Hunger was a symptom. Something deeper was wrong.

That was the moment I decided I wouldn't let him disappear the way so many kids did. I wouldn't let him fade into another file. Another statistic. Another case closed too early.

The problem was that once I made that decision, I stopped seeing the boundary between protecting him and saving him, and those are not the same thing.

Not at all.

CHAPTER 4
RUTH TO JACK

You think fainting was the worst of it, Jack? It wasn't. That was just the first thing anyone else bothered to notice. They sent him to the nurse, gave him water, told him to rest, and acted like that solved everything. I tried to explain he didn't just fall over. Children don't collapse without a reason. Not the way he did.

Nobody cared. Nobody listened.

I kept trying. Meetings. Emails. Notes in files nobody read. Every time I pushed, they pushed back harder. They told me I was making a simple issue complicated. They told me to trust the system. They told me to focus on my classroom and let the professionals handle the rest.

The professionals didn't handle anything.

By the time they took me seriously, it was already too late.

I wish I meant too late for Daniel. I don't. I mean too late for me.

I had already crossed the line in my head. I had already decided I wasn't going to let him get swallowed like every other child the school failed to protect.

You want to know why they called me the Lunchbox Lady? Fine. I'll give you the real version. You're the only one up here who actually wants the truth.

So listen carefully. This next part is the reason everything broke.

CHAPTER 5
RUTH

After Daniel fainted, I started packing extra lunches. Not snacks. Full meals with sandwiches, fruit, vegetables, and juice. I labeled the bags with nothing but a small initial so no one would think they were special. If anyone noticed I was bringing more food than usual, they didn't say anything.

Daniel accepted the lunches quietly. He didn't ask questions. He didn't thank me. He just ate them with the same careful, deliberate chewing he used with the food from home.

Nothing in him changed. Not the tension in his shoulders. Not the way he flinched at loud sounds. Not the way he tracked the door. He wasn't starving anymore, but he wasn't safe either.

I kept watching. That was my mistake. Once you start watching a child who's slipping, you can't unsee it. You start keeping count—missed assignments, unexplained bruises, sudden shifts in mood, days where they come in wearing the same clothes as the day before, patterns you've seen a hundred times.

I knew what was happening. I couldn't prove it. Those two realities rarely line up at the same time.

I called his mother again. She told me he was being dramatic.

She said she had raised three children already and didn't need a teacher telling her how to handle the fourth. She hung up on me. I knew then that she wasn't going to help him. I knew I was on my own.

The school warned me not to intervene again. They reminded me of boundaries. They talked about liability. They talked about "appropriate concern," which is the same phrase people use when they don't want you to interfere but don't want to look responsible if something goes wrong.

I didn't care. I knew Daniel needed someone to step in.

One morning, he came in without a lunchbox at all. I reached into my drawer, took out one of the meals I had brought, and set it on his desk during morning work. He stared at it for a long time before touching it.

At recess, he didn't run. He sat alone near the corner of the fence with his knees pulled to his chest. I walked over under the pretense of supervising the playground. He didn't speak, but he didn't move away either. That was more connection than I had seen from him in weeks.

I asked him if everything was all right at home. He didn't answer. He didn't nod or shake his head. He just kept breathing like it took effort.

Later that afternoon, he told another student he wished he didn't have to go home. The child repeated it to me. She wasn't trying to cause trouble. Children don't understand the weight of those words. They just share what they hear.

I documented that too. Nobody responded.

That was when I started to feel the same thing I used to feel every time one of my former students ended up on the news for something preventable—anger and helplessness. The world was failing someone in real time, and all I was allowed to do was watch.

I made a decision I can't take back.

I stopped waiting for the system to get involved, and I started planning. I told myself it wasn't drastic. I told myself it was temporary. I told myself I wasn't going to let him disappear into another long shadow of neglect.

I decided I would keep him safe.

The problem was simple. Once I believed that, everything else became too easy.

CHAPTER 6
RUTH TO JACK

You want the part everyone twists around, the part they call kidnapping, the part they act like I planned for weeks. It wasn't like that. It was one decision made after too many days of watching a child walk into a building looking smaller than the day before.

I didn't grab him off the street. I didn't drag him out a window. I didn't lure him anywhere. I did what I had always done. I fed him. I talked to him. I made sure he felt seen, and when the moment came, he stepped toward me on his own.

The world keeps forgetting that part.

The school called it abduction. His mother called it interference.

I think she said what she did because she needed someone to blame besides herself.

The district called it misconduct because they didn't want to deal with the fact that every warning sign was in their files long before I ever crossed a line.

You want my version, Jack? Fine. I'll give you exactly what I did, and I'll give you the part that mattered most, the part none of them understood. I didn't take him away. I took him out of the path of something he couldn't outrun.

CHAPTER 7
RUTH

The day everything broke started like any other—morning work, handwriting practice, and a lesson on telling time. Daniel sat as straight as usual, keeping one eye on the door. His lunchbox was missing again. He didn't look surprised.

I had packed an extra meal, but I didn't put it on his desk right away. I waited to see if he would ask for help, but he didn't. He just kept working with that rigid concentration children use when they're trying not to crumble.

At recess, he didn't join the others. He stood near the fence, watching the parking lot like he expected someone to appear.

When I came closer, he didn't move. He whispered something under his breath, too soft for anyone else to notice. I stepped beside him and asked if he wanted to stay inside for the last ten minutes. He nodded.

Inside the classroom, he sat at the reading table. I brought out his lunch. He stared at it before touching it. When he finally did, he ate as though he was worried someone would take it from him.

The bell rang, and the other children returned. Daniel looked toward the door again. His face changed in a way I hadn't seen before, like the air had thickened around him. I followed his gaze.

His mother was standing in the hallway, and she wasn't smiling. Her presence made the entire room feel smaller.

She motioned for him, and he flinched. I don't mean a subtle hesitation. I mean his shoulders jerked as though someone had struck him. The children noticed. I noticed. She didn't.

That was the moment. The decision. The line.

His mother repeated the motion, sharper this time. I stepped between them without thinking. I told her he wasn't feeling well and needed a few minutes. She pushed past me and grabbed his arm. His face went blank in a way no eight-year-old's face should ever look.

I felt something snap in me. Not anger. Not fear.

Certainty.

I told her to let go. She didn't. She pulled him harder, and he didn't resist. That was the worst part. He moved the way children move when they've learned resistance only makes things worse.

I told her I had concerns about his safety. She called me dramatic and said I had always been dramatic. She said Daniel needed discipline, not attention and dragged him toward the door.

I followed. I didn't shout. I didn't cause a scene. I simply reached for him, and he stepped toward me instead of her.

She froze.

I took his hand. I told her he needed help.

She told me to mind my own business.

So I made him my business.

I walked him back into the classroom, shut the door, and locked it. He didn't cry. He didn't panic. He sat at the reading table with his palms flat, breathing in short, sharp bursts. He looked at me like he didn't know whether he was in trouble or safe.

I told him I wasn't going to let anything bad happen to him.

I didn't try to run. I didn't hide him. I stayed in the room with him until the police arrived. They ordered me to open the door, so

I did. They asked me what I thought I was doing. I told them exactly what I believed—that I was trying to protect a child.

They didn't see it that way. They never do.

Daniel was led out of the room by two officers. His mother followed them. He didn't look back. That part stays with me.

The school suspended me that afternoon. The district fired me by the end of the week. The investigation called me unstable, inappropriate, and dangerous. They twisted my judgment into something unrecognizable. They ignored every warning sign I had reported for months.

They said I crossed a line, and they were right, but they never asked me why. They never asked what I saw. They never asked who Daniel became when the door closed behind him.

I was the only one who cared enough to act, and in the end, that was what sealed my fate.

CHAPTER 8
JACK

Ruth sits still after she finishes. Not calm. Not relieved. Just still. It's like talking put her back into that classroom. Some patients drift after a confession. She doesn't. She stays anchored.

"I did what I thought was right," she says once, her voice barely loud enough to register. "That's the part nobody forgives."

I don't answer. I've learned not to step in between a person and their own regrets. It never helps. It only turns the room into a courtroom, and that's not my job.

Outside her room, the generator kicks on again. The lights flicker hard enough to make the hallway feel thinner.

The blizzard pushes against the windows like it wants in. Half the ward is asleep, half pretending to be, and the handful of us workers are counting hours we weren't meant to be here for.

Ruth calls after me before I reach the door. "Do you think I hurt him?"

I stop but don't turn around. You can't lie in this place. People feel it.

"You hurt yourself," I say. "He was already hurt before you ever stepped in."

She takes that in without fighting it. That alone tells me everything I need to know.

"Do you know why they sent me here? To this place?" she asks.

I shake my head.

"Daniel was the youngest child of a big name judge. I was sent here to be erased. Do you think anyone will tell the family I'm gone?"

I shake my head. The warden didn't ask me for her confession, so I think if she were sent here to be erased, it worked.

NIGHT 10: CHRISTOPHER

CHRISTOPHER INTRO

Someone from day shift taped paper stars to the elevator doors. Half of them fell by the time I came on.

Tonight's patient is Christopher Dane, forty-five. Former firefighter. Burn scars across one arm, and a stare trained on exits more than faces.

People think firefighters fear fire. They don't. They fear the moment after, when the choices settle in.

His transfer notes say "moral fatigue." That's what administrators write when they don't want to say survivor's guilt out loud.

He watched something burn.

He watched someone not come out.

He's ready to explain why he let the flames answer for him.

Night Ten.

This one's going to hurt.

CHAPTER 1
JACK

Someone from day shift taped paper stars to the elevator doors. Half of them are lying on the floor now. Cheap tape doesn't hold against the cold, and whoever put them should've known that. Nothing flimsy lasts up here.

December in these parts is finicky, but it's always cold and full of snow. Some years, the blizzards are feracious. There's no blizzard right now, but the temperature has dropped again.

The vents push out air that's warm near the ceiling but cold at the floor. You can stand in one place and feel two different temperatures.

Tonight's patient is a late transfer. Christopher Dane is sixty-five. He's a former firefighter and has burn scars across half his body.

You get used to where people aim their eyes. Some track the meds. Others track the restraints. Christopher tracks every door, every hallway corner, and every sprinkler head in the ceiling.

People like to say firefighters are brave, but they forget that bravery is just another word for walking into places everyone else is running away from.

His transfer notes said "moral fatigue." I think it should be called what it is—survivor's guilt.

According to his file, he did his share of hero work—multiple rescues, commendations, community events. He had the kind of career they put on recruitment posters. After one night, one call, one house, everything fell apart.

Not really sure why he was sent here, but maybe we'll find out tonight.

The official report said he followed protocol. The investigation said the conditions made further entry unsafe. The department cleared him.

The family didn't, and neither did he.

He sits on the edge of the bed when I walk in, his feet flat, his hands on his knees. No restraints. Who's fucked up idea was that?

A monitor and a line run into his good arm. The burned one is mottled and twisted from wrist to elbow, a patchwork of old heat and skin grafts.

He watches me then the door then the window that covers in frost. He looks like a man who still expects to hear alarms at any second, even in a place where alarms just mean someone's heart has given up.

He signed the consent for a recorded conversation when he first came to Death Ward. The warden likes those on file, especially when a patient comes in with a reputation. The news called Christopher a lot of things—hero, coward, broken. They rotated the words depending on the day. No one asked him which one fit.

I wonder if he even knows.

He watches me pull up the chair. He knows what this is.

"This one's going to hurt," I say, mostly to myself.

Christopher doesn't flinch. He just starts talking.

CHAPTER 2
CHRISTOPHER TO JACK

You know what people always ask first, Jack? They don't ask what it smelled like, or how hot it was, or how long it took for the roof to go. They ask one question every time.

"Did you try?"

They want a simple answer—yes or no. They want to sort you into a box—hero or coward, action or failure. They don't want to sit in the part in between because that's where the real damage is.

I got used to answering it. "Yes, we tried. Yes, we went in. Yes, we made entry. Yes, we followed procedure. Yes, we checked the rooms we could reach. Yes, we backed out when the structure started to fail."

It was all true. It just wasn't the whole truth.

The whole truth is that "trying" isn't a single decision. It's a chain of them. You know that. You see it up here every night. People don't just end up in beds like this because of one moment. It's the way every small choice lines up.

I became a firefighter for the same reason a lot of us do. I wanted to be the one going in instead of the one standing on the sidewalk. I thought that would make life simpler. You see danger, you move toward it, you pull someone out, and you go home. Clean story.

It isn't clean. It never was.

They dressed it up with words like duty and service, and I believed them. Then, you do enough calls, and you start to notice that sometimes, you don't go in as far as you could. Sometimes, you hear something, and you tell yourself you didn't. Sometimes, you look at a doorway and think "if I step through that, neither of us is coming back," and you step somewhere else instead.

They don't put that on the posters.

You want to know why I'm here? Everyone else acts like it's because of one person who didn't make it out, but that's not it. I've lost people before. More than I like to admit. You can't do this work without stacking up ghosts.

I'm here because of who I decided didn't deserve my last effort. I picked who the fire would take, and I need you to hear exactly how I did it.

CHAPTER 3
CHRISTOPHER

I joined the department when I was twenty-three. I passed the physical, the written exam, and the psych eval. They asked why I wanted the job. I gave a standard answer. I wanted to help, to make a difference, to be there on someone's worst day and give them a chance to see another one.

They liked that. They heard sincerity, and it checked the right boxes.

The first real structure fire I went to was a single-story house that had already been burning for too long. By the time we got there, the smoke was banking low out of the windows. Flames were visible under the eaves. Neighbors were in the yard yelling about a dog and an old man who might still be inside.

I did what I was trained to do—mask on, hose line in, stay low, follow the wall, and check the rooms.

The first thing that hit me wasn't fear. It was heat. The second was the noise. Fire isn't quiet. It eats and moves and pushes the air around in ways that don't make sense unless you've been inside enough times to understand it.

We found the old man in the hallway, collapsed halfway between his bedroom and the front door. We dragged him out while another crew found the dog under the kitchen table. The dog was barely breathing as they brought him out onto the yard. Medics worked on the man. Someone soaked the dog with water and wrapped it in a towel. The crowd cheered when the dog coughed.

The old man died on the way to the hospital, but the dog lived.

That was my first lesson—people don't know where to put their grief, so they latch onto whatever survives. If it's an animal, they act like that balances the scales. It doesn't.

After that, the calls blurred. Car wrecks. Kitchen fires. Faulty space heaters. Overloaded outlets. Kids playing with lighters. You learn patterns fast. You see the same mistakes repeated in different houses. You stop being surprised by how many people think smoke will wake you up before it kills you.

The first time I carried a child out of a burning building, I was thirty. It was from a third-floor apartment filled with heavy smoke, the mother screaming on the lawn. We'd already pulled one kid from a bedroom closet. The second was under the bed in the next room, wedged in so tightly I had to drag him out by his ankles. He was limp in my arms. For a few seconds, I thought he was gone.

He wasn't. He started coughing on the stairs as we came down. By the time we hit the grass, he was crying. I've never been so grateful for the sound of a child crying in my life.

That made the paper. There was a photo. My gear was black with soot, my mask off, the kid in my arms. People in the background clapped. They loved that picture. They put it on the station wall. They called me a hero for weeks.

I let them.

They didn't know I'd walked past a closed door in that hallway because the heat was bad and my partner was yelling that we needed to back out. We were following the line. We were watching the ceiling. We were doing what we'd been trained to do when conditions shift from risky to dangerous.

I always wondered what was behind that door. The investigators said no one was home. The fire pattern backed that up. Still, the thought planted itself and stayed.

That's how this works. You have the official version, and then you have the one that plays in your head at three in the morning.

There were other calls—some good, some awful. A warehouse fire where the sprinklers failed. A nursing home evacuation where we got everyone out but one man who refused to leave his roommate's side. A teenager who set his own room on fire and then changed his mind too late.

I stacked up names and faces. I also stacked up choices. In or out. Push or pull. Break the window or leave it. Go left or right. You think you'll always make the brave choice, but you don't. Sometimes the brave choice is the wrong one.

The night that matters most didn't start out any different than any other.

It was December. Cold. We were decorating the bay with cheap lights. Somebody brought in cookies from his wife. The radio was quiet in that way that always makes you nervous. You start thinking maybe you'll get through the night without anything big, and that's when the tones drop.

House fire. Residential. Possible entrapment. We rolled out like we always did.

The address was familiar before we pulled onto the street. I recognized the block. We'd been there before. Not for fire. For a wellness check when a neighbor called about yelling and crashes and a kid crying for too long.

We'd walked into that particular house twice already that year —once for a woman with a bruised cheek and a split lip who told us she'd fallen and once for a boy with a broken wrist who said he had slipped on the stairs. The man in the house had insisted everything was fine both times. He was the sort who filled a room just by standing in it. He was angry without raising his voice.

We documented. We handed information to the right people. We left. But nothing changed.

When we turned the corner that night, the house was already

venting fire through a blown-out window on the second floor. Smoke rolled over the roof. Neighbors were in the yard again. The same boy stood on the sidewalk in bare feet, his coat half on. He was shaking. The woman was nowhere in sight.

I stepped off the truck. You learn to read a scene fast. Fire location, wind direction, structural clues… they all hit you at once.

The boy pointed at the house. "Dad's inside," he said.

That was the moment the real story started.

CHAPTER 4
CHRISTOPHER TO JACK

You've heard enough of these to know the next part usually goes one of two ways—either I tell you I ran in without thinking and something went wrong or I tell you I hesitated and something went wrong. Both sound tragic. Both make sense to people who've never done the job.

That's not what happened.

We didn't rush in blindly. We did what we were trained to do. I masked up. My partner masked up. We went in low. Heat banked off the ceiling. Visibility was garbage, but I'd been in worse.

We found fire in the kitchen and knocked it back enough to move past. The stairs were still intact. We started up, following the wall and checking doors—standard search pattern.

I want you to understand something before I tell you the rest. I knew that house. I knew that family. We all did. We'd been warned to be careful with the father. "History of aggression," they called it. "Uncooperative." "Unstable when intoxicated."

I also knew the boy had been outside when we pulled up. I knew the woman was missing. I knew the only person whose location nobody could confirm was the man who hurt them.

I knew all of that.

And then I heard him.

Upstairs. Down the hall. Behind a closed door. Not calling for help. Not calling for his son. Shouting. Cursing. Slamming into something.

There are moments when time stretches. You know the ones. It's when you feel every possible version of the next ten seconds branching out in front of you. You pick one, and the others don't vanish. They just go live somewhere else in your head.

I knew if I went to that door, I was putting myself and my partner in more danger. He might fight us, he might drag us off balance, he might refuse to leave, and we would have to choose between forcing him or saving his wife before the place turned into a collapse zone.

I also knew, very clearly, that there was a part of me that didn't want to save him.

You can write that down.

I'd seen the bruise on his wife's cheek. I'd heard the way his son flinched at his voice. I'd stood in that doorway before and watched him plaster on a fake smile while something mean simmered underneath. I knew what kind of man he was.

Fire doesn't care. It just burns. It doesn't weigh sins. It doesn't check reports. It doesn't choose.

That night, I did.

You want the details. You're not going to get smoke and flames from me. That's not the part that matters. What matters is that I heard him in that room, and I turned away.

The truth is simpel. I decided the house could have him, and I've been standing in that hallway ever since.

CHAPTER 5
CHRISTOPHER

We hit the top of the stairs and found the first door on the left open. A bedroom. No one was on the bed, no one on the floor. I swept under it with my hand out of habit. Nothing. Heat was building, but it was still manageable.

The shouting came from farther down the hall. A man's voice, hoarse and furious. He was yelling words I didn't need to understand. The tone was enough. I heard something crash. Furniture. Glass. Maybe both.

My partner glanced toward the sound through the gray, but I kept moving to the next door. I told myself we were following the plan—clear left, clear right, move in order. Don't get drawn toward the noise until you've checked for the silent ones.

That's what they teach you—the quiet victims are the ones who die first, the ones who can't call out, the ones too low on air or consciousness to do anything but wait.

We opened the next door. A bathroom. Empty. The mirror was already fogged, the air thick. The fire had gained ground somewhere above or behind the walls. I could feel it.

He must have heard us because he started yelling louder now for us to get out, to leave, to mind our own business. There was a solid sound, like a shoulder hitting wood. The door shook.

I put my hand on the knob and felt the heat through my glove. Not enough to flash but enough to warn me the room was compromised.

I pictured him on the other side—angry, drunk, maybe injured, maybe not, maybe with a weapon, maybe just with two fists and enough rage to make him unpredictable.

I could hear my captain in my head from training years earlier. "No hero work. You go home at the end of your shift. You don't trade three lives for one man who doesn't want saving."

I stepped past the door.

We reached the last room on the hall. The door was half open. Inside, the floor felt wrong. It was spongy, as though something beneath had already burned through. We did a quick sweep from the threshold, staying low and checking behind the furniture as best we could without committing to full entry. No bodies. No movement. No one hiding in the corners.

The smoke thickened. My low-air alarm started to chirp. My partner's did too. We'd been inside longer than it felt.

The radio crackled in my ear. A voice from outside told us conditions were worsening, reminding us we had a kid out on the sidewalk who needed his parents living if possible, accounted for if not. Standard language.

We started back toward the stairs.

The man in the room was still shouting. His voice cracked in the middle of a curse. That was the first time it sounded like fear instead of rage. It cut through me more than I like to admit.

I could have stopped. I could have turned. I could have ordered my partner to brace while I forced the door or at least take a look. I had enough air for one more short push.

But I didn't do it. I kept walking.

On the stairs, the house talked to us in the language we understood—groaning beams, popping nails, and the deep, unsettling sound of heat rearranging structure. It was time to get out.

We exited through the front, our masks still on, steam rolling off our gear. The cold hit my face when I broke seal. I pulled the mask up and caught my breath.

The boy was still on the sidewalk. The neighbor had put a coat on him. He stood there watching the house, his eyes too wide and too dry.

"Is he out?" the neighbor asked. Meaning the man. Meaning the father.

I didn't answer.

The windows failed one by one. Flames rolled along the ceiling inside then pushed out into the open night. The roof sagged near the center. The crew outside knocked down what they could from a defensive position. We weren't going back in. Everyone knew it. No one said it out loud.

We waited for the call from the investigators. We waited for someone to tell us they'd found the mother's car gone from the driveway or if she was somewhere else in town, safe or not. We waited for someone to confirm that the man had left before we'd arrived, that the shouting we'd heard was a television or a neighbor or our own imaginations.

They didn't.

He was found two days later during overhaul on the second floor behind the door we'd walked past.

The report said he'd likely been intoxicated. It noted signs of struggle inside the room—broken furniture and blood on the wall where he'd hit his head before being overcome. It mentioned the location of the body and the proximity to a partially open window he could have used to escape.

The conclusion stated that given fire conditions at the time of entry and the risk to personnel, further rescue attempts beyond established search pattern would not have been justified.

It cleared us.

The family didn't clear us. The boy didn't. The mother didn't. She looked at the house then at us and asked a different question.

"Did he suffer?"

We told her what we were allowed to say—smoke inhalation, loss of consciousness, quick, painless. The usual words.

She shook her head like she knew better.

The department moved on. Calls kept coming. Houses kept burning. People kept needing help. I kept responding.

But something had changed.

Every scene after that, I saw doors. Every call, I heard voices I didn't go to. Every time we backed out, I wondered who was behind the one door we didn't force open.

You can get used to physical pain. You can rehab an injury. You can learn to live with scars.

But you can't rehab a choice.

I started waking up at night hearing him. Not shouting this time. Not cursing. Just breathing hard on the other side of a door while I walked away.

My hands shook on the steering wheel when I drove home from shift. I stopped staying for coffee at the station. I stopped going to the bar with the crew. I stopped visiting houses where we'd made good saves. I didn't want balance. I didn't want the word "hero" anymore. It felt like an accusation every time someone used it.

I went on leave after I froze at a kitchen fire six months later. It was just a small blaze, a grease fire on a stove. We could see the flames from the window. It should have been routine.

It wasn't. I hesitated on the porch. Just a second. Just long enough for my captain to notice and push past me to take the nozzle. No one was hurt. The fire went out. The family was grateful.

I couldn't shake the knowledge that I'd hesitated in the easiest possible scenario. If I hesitated there, what would I do when something big came again?

I knew the answer. I'd already given it once.

I went home. I didn't go back.

CHAPTER 6
CHRISTOPHER TO JACK

You've heard the official version now — the report, the chain of events, the parts that make sense to people who've never had to pick a direction in smoke.

But that's not the confession, Jack, not entirely.

The confession is this — I didn't just decide to let a violent man stay behind. I decided I knew what he deserved. I decided I was qualified to weigh his life against the risk to mine. I decided the fire could do what the courts hadn't.

You can call it triage. You can call it survival. You can call it instinct.

I call it playing judge in a room where nobody asked me to wear the robe.

You work here. You see what people are capable of. You hear what they've done. You've probably wondered if the world might be better off without some of them. Don't bother denying it. You're human.

The difference between you and me is that you didn't stand in a hallway with the power to walk toward or away. You just sit in a chair and listen after the fact.

I turned away while I still had air in my tank. That's the part I can't live with.

Everybody tells me the same things. "You didn't have time." "You followed procedure." "You couldn't save everyone." "You don't know if he would have made it out anyway."

All true, but none of it matters.

Because I know I heard him. I know I could have tried. I know I weighed him and found him lacking.

And here's the quiet part I never told the investigators—I wasn't completely wrong about him, but I was wrong about who else might be in that room.

They found a second plate on the nightstand. But no body. No remains. No proof. Just signs that someone smaller had been there not long before the fire.

The boy swore he'd been alone when he'd run out. The mother said the daughter had been with her that night. Records backed them up. On paper, there was no missing child.

But I saw the blanket in the photograph, and I've never been sure who I left behind that door.

That uncertainty is worse than any verdict.

You want to know why I'm on your floor instead of living out a quiet retirement? It's simple.

I see flames now. Every room I'm in is on fire. I used to go batshit crazy because of this.

Is that in my file? Every room I'm in, flames lick the walls, but they never come close to me. They never claim me.

Why is that?

CHAPTER 7
JACK

Some confessions come out twisted. You have to dig through excuses and self-pity to find the real thing. Christopher's didn't. He laid it all out like a report—chronological, organized, brutal in how straightforward it was.

He didn't cry. He didn't shake. His voice didn't break. If anything, he sounded like a man giving a training lecture on what not to do.

"That's it," he says when he's done. "That's the hallway I never left."

I don't bother telling him he had. His body had, anyway. The rest of him is still standing there, listening to a door he never opened.

Survivor's guilt is a phrase people throw around when they're uncomfortable. It sounds clinical and controlled. It belongs in a handbook.

Moral fatigue is even worse. It makes the whole thing sound like a long day on the job instead of what it really is—a life you can't put down.

"Do you think he deserved it?" Christopher asks after a while. "The man. Be honest."

I thought about all the files I'd read over the years. Men who hurt children. Men who hurt women. Men who kept doing it, no matter how many chances they got. I thought about the burns on Christopher's arm, the boy on the sidewalk, the bruise on the wife's face.

"Doesn't matter what I think," I say. "The fire already gave its verdict."

He snorts at that. Not amused. Just acknowledging the line.

"I keep waiting for someone to tell me I did the right thing," he says.

"That's not my job," I tell him. "I'm here to listen. I'm here to help make sure your last moments aren't too painful."

"And then what?" he asks. "What do you do with what I said? Lock it in a drawer?"

"Something like that," I say.

He leans back and looks at the line in his arm. "It won't hurt?"

"No more than it does now."

He nods and closes his eyes. "Make it quick before the flames reach me. Please?"

I make it quick.

When I leave the room, the hallway feels warmer than usual. The vents rattle like they are pushing more heat than the building needs. One of the paper stars on the elevator falls as I walk past. I pick it up without thinking and stick it back on the metal. It falls again.

On my way back to the desk, I watch the exit signs over each door. The green rectangles are steady and quiet. Christopher would have noticed them all. Some habits never fade.

Here's what I learned tonight—people think firefighters are afraid of fire. They're wrong. It's the empty doorway that haunts them

NIGHT 11: JENNA

JENNA INTRO

Tonight's patient is Jenna Cross, thirty-four. Former hospice volunteer.

Her file says "pattern interference." Means she inserted herself into deaths she wasn't assigned to. Means she liked being the last voice people heard.

She keeps asking me if the lights can be dimmer.

They're already dim.

But people who want to disappear rarely know how visible they are.

Night Eleven.

Time to hear why she made herself indispensable to strangers who never asked.

CHAPTER 1
JACK

The ward smells like peppermint. Again.

The day shift brought in hot cocoa in a crockpot and left it behind. Ike decided to spike it with a little something "extra." Again. Like he does every year.

I'm not saying I mind, but I am keeping an eye on how much everyone drinks. It's a good thing we have a very quiet floor tonight.

Tonight's patient is Jenna Cross. She's sixty-four, a former hospice volunteer.

"I think you should sit with her tonight." Ike says.

"What the hell for?"

He shrugs, "for shits and giggles."

"She's not on my list." She never has been.

"Why's that? Hit too close to home maybe?"

I tell him to fuck off. His reply is to fill my mug with the hot cocoa and then hand me Jenna's file. "She's waiting."

Some days, I hate him, but it's his turn to pay the bar tab so tonight, I pretend to like him.

And if you're inserting an eye roll here, I don't blame you. The asshole is my best friend, but talking with Jenna tonight is not something I want to do. If you must know, he's right. Her story does hit too close to home.

When I step into Jenna's room, she's lying there with her eyes closed. Her left hand is wrapped around a pair of My Little Pony sunglasses, which I'm assuming one of the staff gave her. There's a note in her file that her eyes are sensitive, and she prefers to stay in the dark.

I'm not sure if she has light sensitivity or if she's trying to hide.

People don't realize that the more they try to disappear, the more visible to others they are.

Her hair is pulled back in a loose braid. Her voice, when she uses it, has always been quiet enough to make you lean forward even though you don't want to. I think it's because she was used to speaking softly around the dying. Some never turn the volume back up.

She watches me the way someone watches a grieving family—measured, patient, and waiting to be needed.

There's the problem—I don't need her.

I pull my chair up close. It scrapes on the floor.

She doesn't flinch. She just starts talking before I even have the chance to say hello.

CHAPTER 2
JENNA TO JACK

I was told you'd be showing up. What's in the cup? It smells good. Any way I could have a sip of that?

No? Doesn't hurt to ask.

I was told you'd be wanting my story. Is that true? I've heard about your famous deals, but you've never mentioned it to me. Is it too late? Or is that why you're here?

I promise I'll make it a good one. I'll share some secrets with you.

You know, you and I are a lot alike. We both take care of the dying. Well, at least, I used to. We're death angels, you and I. In that, we share a bond.

You, of all people, should understand why I did what I did. I shouldn't have to explain it to you, but maybe that's why you're here now. You're the perfect person to listen, aren't you?

I can start anywhere, but I'll start here—people think dying is loud, but it isn't. It's quieter than anything else. It's the quiet that gets inside your head.

Does it get in yours?

That's what started it for me. Not death. Not grief. The quiet.

When I volunteered, they told us our job was to offer comfort. That's it. We were to accompany, not guide. To sit and not speak unless spoken to.

Most people follow that. I tried. I really tried.

But you don't understand what it's like to watch someone slip and know you could steady them even for one breath, if you just said the right thing. You do that here. You understand more than you admit.

You want the real version, not the one in the file. So listen. I didn't interfere because I wanted attention. I interfered because I knew when someone didn't want to die alone.

Eventually, I learned how to tell who didn't want to die at all.

I know you know what I'm saying, Jack. You know the signs too.

CHAPTER 3
JENNA

The first hospice room I ever walked into was too warm. Someone had turned the thermostat up as high as it would go, no doubt because the woman in the bed was eighty-six and probably had complained she was freezing. Her daughter sat in the corner, staring at her phone with the desperation of someone who couldn't bring herself to look at the bed.

I was supposed to sit quietly, and I did.

The woman opened her eyes once. Her mouth moved, but nothing came out. I watched her chest rise in a short rhythm then fall again. The space between the breaths grew longer. The daughter didn't notice. Or maybe she couldn't notice.

I leaned forward in the chair just enough to see the woman's face. There was fear there. Not of dying. Of being left. It was the fear you see in children who wake up from nightmares and call for someone who doesn't come right away.

I whispered that I was there. The daughter didn't look up, but the woman heard me. Her eyes shifted in my direction, and her breathing steadied. I didn't touch her. I didn't break a rule. I just spoke, and she wasn't afraid anymore.

She died ten minutes later.

People said I had a gift, but that's not what I would call it. It's not a gift to listen. It's not a gift to understand and to empathize. That's basic human nature. I will always remember the fear in her face and how it changed when she realized she wasn't alone. That stayed with me.

The next patient was a man in his sixties with cancer that had spread everywhere. He was angry that day. He said no one listened to him, that the staff rushed him. He said the world moved too fast around someone who couldn't move at all.

He told me he wasn't ready, that he needed more time. He just wanted to wait until his sister arrived so that he wouldn't be alone.

I wasn't supposed to answer, but I did anyway. I told him I heard him, and he calmed immediately. He died the next morning.

His sister arrived twenty minutes later.

That was the moment I realized something important—most people don't get what they want at the end, but they still try to ask for it. They whisper it. They hope someone catches it.

Most people never do.

I started listening more carefully, not just for words but for patterns, for the hesitation in their voice, for the way a breath sounded when someone was holding back something heavier than fear.

Patterns told the truth better than charts.

Soon, I wasn't just volunteering on my assigned visits. I stayed longer, and I returned after hours. I would slip into rooms where the staff said families weren't coming.

I told myself it was compassion, and sometimes, it was, but sometimes, it was something else.

I learned how to tell when someone was fighting the end and when someone was calling for it.

Once I understood that difference, I couldn't stop, and that was when everything began to fall apart.

CHAPTER 4
JENNA TO JACK

You're wondering when it shifted, when I went from helping to harming, aren't you?

That's what everyone wants to know. Where the line is. Where it snapped.

But there wasn't a snap. There was drift.

I didn't walk into rooms thinking I had some mystical power or that I was the one in control of when someone dies... unlike you.

I walked in because no one else was there.

I walked in because I could understand what those in the beds needed before anyone else noticed.

You've seen it on this floor. Someone reaches the end of a long road, and the room goes cold, and there's a quiet that wasn't there before.

Death waits, and the silence is deathly.

I listened for that difference, and then I acted on it.

They called that interference.

I'll tell you who I helped and who I stayed with when I shouldn't have. I'll even tell you why I couldn't stop, but understand this first—I never touched anyone. I never pushed. I never pulled. I never made something happen that wasn't going to happen in the first place.

I just chose who shouldn't die alone and who shouldn't die yet.

That choice was enough to ruin me.

CHAPTER 5
JENNA

I started keeping my own list, not a formal one, just notes I made after each visit. My list contained things like patterns and warnings. I'd include things the staff didn't notice because they were busy managing medications, families, emergencies, and paperwork.

A lot can be missed when you're busy focusing on other things.

There was a young woman with congestive heart failure who cried only when the lights were turned off, an old man with dementia who kept asking if his wife was waiting for him, a middle-aged man with ALS who mouthed "not yet" every time someone tried to comfort him, and then there was a woman with terminal lymphoma who begged for someone to hold her hand but only after visitors left the room.

I wasn't assigned to all of them.

The hospice coordinator told us to stay in our lanes and only go where we were assigned. We were to document everything, leave when our time was up, and say nothing personal.

Most important, we listen, but we don't guide. We don't encourage someone to go to sleep, follow the light, or anything else that might seem like we were encouraging their death.

I broke every rule.

When I saw someone slipping sooner than expected, I stayed longer. When I saw someone fighting the last breath, I whispered to them, and when I saw someone who needed someone present, I sat near their bed.

It wasn't dramatic. It wasn't unethical.

Not yet.

But then I met Thomas.

He was forty-eight. His kidneys were failing. His heart was struggling, and he had no family, no visitors. It's like he was forgotten about.

Here's the thing about Thomas. He wasn't afraid of dying. He was afraid no one would know he was gone.

He told me he wanted someone to say his name just once after he passed. He asked me to do it, and so I did.

Was that wrong? Not to me. It felt like the bare minimum of what another human being could do.

He died at 2:17 a.m. The nurse on duty was busy with another patient.

He looked at me right before his last breath, and I knew he wasn't scared. He was just waiting, so I said his name, and he let go.

After him, I couldn't go back to sitting quietly in a corner hoping someone else would fill the gap.

Instead, I filled it, and the more gaps I filled, the less I trusted the system around me to catch anything at all.

That's when I started entering rooms at night when I wasn't scheduled. Not every night, just the nights where the silence felt wrong. The silence wasn't frightening but not peaceful either.

An absence instead of a rest.

The hospice staff trusted volunteers, probably a little too much. They let us sign in without checking if we stayed in our assigned rooms, and they assumed we followed protocol because that was what volunteers were supposed to do.

I didn't.

I found the rooms where the feeling was thick, the ones where death hovered too far or too close, where someone was holding their breath for help and nobody else noticed.

Sometimes, I sat in the dark at the foot of a bed and waited. Sometimes, I whispered to someone who could no longer respond. Sometimes, I stayed until morning so the nurse would think I'd been scheduled there.

The pattern grew slowly, not because I wanted it to but because I couldn't ignore it anymore.

Death is predictable until it isn't, and I started seeing every exception.

The hospice director called it a boundary issue. The nurses called it strange. The families called it comforting or creepy depending on what they believed luck meant.

I didn't care what they called it. I cared about what the dying needed and what the nearly dying tried to say without words.

The trouble came with Meredith.

She was thirty-nine with a brain tumor. She was beautiful even after weeks of decline. She was also married, and they had one child.

Her husband visited every morning, her mother every evening. Her sister came on weekends, but Meredith didn't speak her fears when they were there. She saved those words for the quiet hours after midnight, for whoever stayed when everyone else had gone home.

I was the only one who listened.

She told me she was afraid of dying before her daughter's birthday, that she wanted to hold on, but she wasn't sure her body would. Most importantly, she told me she needed someone to tell her it was all right to stay.

Not to go. To stay.

That always stuck with me. I guess her family were telling her it was all right to let go, that they would be okay, but they never asked her what she wanted.

People always assume hospice is about letting go. Sometimes, it's about holding on.

She asked me to keep her awake. Not literally. Emotionally.

She needed someone to talk to, someone who wouldn't cry, someone who wasn't already mourning her, so I stayed with her every night for two weeks. Unassigned, unapproved, and completely against protocol.

She stabilized a little.

Then, the director found out I'd been entering rooms I wasn't assigned to.

They pulled me aside and suspended my shifts. They said they needed to review my behavior and actions, claiming I'd crossed lines. They even said families were noticing my presence "too often."

I begged them to let me see Meredith again, but they denied me. They said she had enough support.

They didn't know what she'd told me or what she'd needed.

She died the night they barred me from her room.

The nurse on duty found her at 4:12 a.m.

Her family thanked the staff, and they told the hospice they were grateful she didn't die alone.

They were wrong.

She did die alone.

That night broke something in me, not because she died but because she died without the one thing she begged for—presence.

After Meredith, I was eventually allowed to volunteer again. I didn't trust anyone—not nurses, not the director, not family members, not the system—to give people what they asked for at the end, so I made sure they got it from me.

Every time. Whether I was assigned to them or not.

CHAPTER 6
JENNA TO JACK

You're waiting for the part where I hurt someone. You think I'm circling around it, but I'm not.

I never laid a hand on anyone. I never sped anything up. I never told someone to stop fighting.

What I did was show up. Even when nobody wanted me to. Even when the staff tried to stop me. Even when families asked for privacy.

I know how that sounds—obsessive, unstable, dangerous.

But nobody asked why I kept going back.

Nobody wanted to know what I heard in those rooms. Nobody wanted to understand what people said when they thought the world had stopped paying attention.

You want the truth? Here it is—some of them weren't ready to die... and some of them weren't dying at all.

CHAPTER 7
JENNA

It started with Mr. Hill. He was seventy-two with congestive heart failure. He was stable one day, confused the next, and then stable again.

The hospice nurse charted "decline expected," but he wasn't declining. He was hovering.

Some people hover. When they hover, they're not improving, but they're also not fading. They are just stuck between two states.

That kind of lingering terrifies staff. It messes with their schedules. It confuses families, and it creates uncertainty. If there's one thing I learned, it's that uncertainty makes people impatient.

The nurse assigned to him started hinting that he was ready to go. Don't get me wrong. She was kind about it, but she said the same phrases over and over. "He's tired." "He's losing ground." "He's showing signs."

I sat with him one night and told him he didn't have to go if he didn't want to.

His eyes focused for the first time in days, not with desperation but with clarity.

He whispered that he wasn't ready, that he still wanted one more conversation with his grandson, but nobody had arranged it. He whispered that he felt pushed.

Pushed. A dying man said he felt pushed.

I stayed longer that night, and yes, it was against rules. That didn't matter to me.

He died two days later.

The nurse charted it as a peaceful death, but I charted it differently in my head.

After him came others, but let me be clear. I was not the one at fault here. Others were.

There was a woman who was given medication too early because she looked uncomfortable even though she was just adjusting in the bed.

There was a man who squeezed my hand with more strength than anyone expected from someone "minutes away."

There was also a young patient with terminal illness whose breathing stabilized when someone simply talked to him.

They weren't dying, but they were being read as dying.

That's not the same at all.

I saw the pattern long before anyone else dared to acknowledge it: Sometimes, staff helped death along because they believed it was compassionate. Sometimes, families hinted at wanting the end to come sooner because they couldn't bear the waiting. Sometimes, the system didn't protect the ones who didn't have voices strong enough to argue.

Once I saw that, I couldn't—wouldn't—stay silent.

I didn't interfere with death. I interfered with decisions others made for the dying.

I didn't save lives. I prolonged them, sometimes by hours, sometimes by days.

I bought people what they needed—time, presence and choice.

That was my crime.

Not speeding anything up. Not harming anyone. Giving them hours they weren't supposed to have.

The hospice director told me I was meddling. The staff told me I didn't understand the "process." The families told administration I made them uncomfortable.

Maybe I did, but none of them were in the rooms at 3 a.m. None of them listened to the way someone's breath changed when their fear eased. None of them heard the whispered last requests because they never bothered to listen.

I did. I kept hearing those patients even when nobody spoke.

The real trouble began when a man stabilized after I stayed with him through the night. He lived two more days, just long enough to say goodbye to someone who would have otherwise arrived too late.

No one outright blamed me, but I was told that I was interfering and causing a nuisance to families. They said I confuse their patients into not accepting death.

I argued and said I was giving them time to welcome it on their terms.

My badge was soon removed, and I was barred from the building. I sat in my car and watched the lights in the hospice wing until dawn, not because I wanted to go back in but because I could feel the silence inside the building.

The wrong kind of silence.

I knew someone was dying. I could feel the shift the same way I always could.

I wasn't there because I wasn't allowed to be, and that was when the real unraveling began.

When you've spent years catching the last breath before it falls, you don't know what to do when you're suddenly told you aren't allowed to.

You hear it anyway. Even across town. Even behind walls. Even with the radio on.

You hear the endings. All of them.

That's what brought me here. Not a crime. Not a violence. A pattern I couldn't shut off once it started.

CHAPTER 8
JENNA TO JACK

People said I'm dangerous. Maybe I am. Not because I hurt anyone but because I noticed too much.

People like me aren't wanted in systems built on routine. We disrupt things. We see where comfort is a cover and where compassion becomes convenience.

You want my final truth, Jack? I wasn't chasing death. I was chasing the moment before it.

That space matters more than the end. Nobody teaches you that. Nobody records it. Nobody honors it.

But I did, and that's why they sent me here.

CHAPTER 9
JACK

Jenna finishes quietly, the same way she started. Her voice didn't rise. Didn't shake. Didn't soften. She delivered her truth like she was reading it from a clipboard she'd already memorized.

She looks at me and asks the question they all eventually ask. "Do you think I crossed lines?"

I don't answer right away. Not because I don't know but because she will take the truth better than a comfort.

"You crossed every line," I say, "but you crossed them for reasons nobody wants to admit exist."

She nods once. Not approval. Not agreement. Just acknowledgment.

"People die here all the time," she says. "Some of them aren't ready."

"I know."

"And some of them would stay if someone held the door open."

"I know that too."

She looks toward the dim lights. "They never let me finish my work."

She closes her eyes. Not in peace. In surrender.

Some people chase the dying. Some chase the moment before. Both lose themselves eventually.

Night Eleven—A volunteer who carried other people's endings until they crushed her.

NIGHT 12: DANIEL

DANIEL INTRO

Last day before Christmas.

Tonight's patient is Daniel Price, forty. Bookkeeper. Ordinary on paper, until you read the line about "holiday ledger event." That's when the numbers stopped being numbers and became reasons.

He keeps adjusting his blanket like someone who's used to tidying small messes instead of large ones. His eyes track every movement in the room, like he's checking if my presence matches my inventory.

He asked one question when I came in:

"Will this change the ending?"

No. But it might change the story.

Night Twelve.

The last confession. Let's make it count.

CHAPTER 1
JACK

It's always crazy on Christmas Eve in this place. It doesn't matter if you are up here on my floor or down below. Music is playing. Christmas cartoons are on the televisions. People are just happy.

We always have a little potluck, and there are always way too many cookies and abandoned cups of eggnog or hot chocolate lying about.

This particular Christmas Eve, I have a patient to sit with while everyone else nibble on sugar cookies and gingerbread men.

I'd already got a call from the warden. He wants the confession tonight. Once you hear who the patient is, you'll understand.

Daniel Price. He's a little famous around here. Daniel looks like any other old man. He would say he was ordinary, living an ordinary life. He was a bookkeeper.

But Daniel Price is not ordinary. Not by a long shot. He's known for the *holiday ledger event*. If you don't know what I'm talking about, I'm not surprised. His infamy was kept out of the news for a reason. The court decided it was safer to pass him to us than to make public what actually happened.

Daniel did books for the kind of people who don't show up on donor lists. Domestic importers. Night clubs with no real business model. A "security firm" that never advertised.

Everyone knew what they were. Daniel knew it better than anyone. Money goes where fear makes it go.

He sits propped up, a blanket over his lap, his fingers smoothing the edge straight. That's the first tell. People who spent their lives fixing small errors don't like crooked lines. His eyes don't stick to me. They move along the walls, the ceiling, the IV pole, and the clipboard at the end of his bed. He doesn't see a room. He sees an inventory.

He asked one question when I came in earlier to check on him. "Will this change the ending?"

No, but it might change the story.

His chart has enough blanks to make the warden nervous. Holiday ledger event is vague on purpose.

This is Night Twelve and our last confession for the year. I saved the best for last.

CHAPTER 2
DANIEL TO JACK

Holiday ledger event... Sounds almost festive, don't you think?

Some people have a lifetime of stories. Some stories take a lifetime to tell.

This is one of them. I had to wait till now. I had to wait until I knew I was going to die on my terms and not someone else's. You know what I mean?

I've been waiting to tell this, so do me a favor, Jack, and don't interrupt. You and I made a deal. I'm honoring my part.

I wasn't just a bookkeeper. I was the bookkeeper for the mob, and let me be clear about something—the numbers were never "just" numbers. They were votes. They were names. They were decisions.

People think men with guns decide who lives and dies. They don't. Men with guns follow orders. The orders come from numbers. From balance sheets. From ledgers.

That was my job. I decided who was worth keeping on the payroll.

You look like you can handle this, so I won't dress it up.

I didn't shoot anybody. I didn't light any fires. I didn't drag anyone into a basement.

I moved decimals. I wrote notes in margins. I flagged "losses."

And people disappeared.

You want to know about Christmas. You want to know why they wrote holiday ledger event instead of what it really was.

So I'll tell you start to finish.

CHAPTER 3
DANIEL

I started doing books for regular people right out of school. Restaurants, car lots, a dentist who didn't understand payroll taxes. People with ties to my family. I was good at it. Not gifted. Just precise.

I liked things that added up. Numbers didn't lie. People did.

The first time I met clients who didn't ask for receipts, it was a bar with no regular hours. Cash only. No signage beyond a first name on the window. The owner didn't care about deductions. He cared about how to describe certain outgoing payments so they didn't bounce back with questions.

He paid on time. He didn't argue. He referred me to friends.

The friends had the same needs. A warehouse listed as storage but never shipping out any product. An events company that never advertised any events. A transport firm with trucks that never showed logged any mileage.

If you do this long enough, you stop pretending. You know who you're working for, and you learn to accept it. You also learn there's no escaping it.

They liked me because I didn't ask questions. I logged what they told me to and matched it against what I saw. If something didn't align, I made it align. That's what they paid for.

I told myself I was just a technician, that I didn't pick targets, that moving numbers around didn't hurt anyone.

Then I caught my first real discrepancy. Not a mistake. Not a typo. A skim.

One of the security guys was pulling cash off the envelopes before they hit the office. Not a lot. Ten here, fifty there. Just enough to call it invisible theft. Over time, it started to show in the logs.

I saw the pattern months before anyone else, but I didn't flag it.

Why would I? It wasn't my skin on the line.

Eventually, the boss—no dramatic title, just Mr. G—asked why the weekly intake didn't match the projections. His voice stayed even. His hands stayed still. Didn't matter. The room got smaller anyway.

I could have thrown the security guy under the bus. I had the reports. I had the slips. I had the math.

Instead, I shrugged and said the usual bullshit.

I blamed it on seasonal dip, on customers tightening belts, on inflation. I blamed it on whatever Mr. G would believe.

I lied.

The skimming continued. The discrepancy grew.

Meanwhile, I watched other things.

I watched who came in late. Who shook when they talked to Mr. G. Who bragged too loudly. Who kept their head down.

Everyone thinks the guys in charge use instinct to pick who needs to go. Sometimes, they do, but mostly, they look at what I hand them and ask one question.

"Is he worth it?"

What they're really asking is, is he worth the risk, worth the cost, and worth the trouble.

That put me in a new position. I wasn't just recording. I was ranking.

I started to realize something ugly. I enjoyed it.

Not the fear. Not the blood.

The control.

You ever sit alone in an office at night with a stack of receipts and know, absolutely know, that the way you interpret those slips will decide who breathes comfortably next month and who starts glancing over their shoulder every time a car slows down near their building?

It's addictive.

I didn't pull the trigger, but when somebody ended up "gone," I could point to the exact line where they became expendable.

That was the prelude.

Then the holidays hit, and everything got busier and uglier at the same time.

CHAPTER 4
DANIEL TO JACK

You've worked nights. You know how December feels in places like this. People get strange. Edges fray. Old guilt wakes up because things are supposed to be warm and meaningful, but they aren't. Not really.

It's the same out there. In my old world, December was bonus season.

Normal companies give out gift cards and ham. Our clients gave out envelopes and "last chances."

Year-end is when you close books. You clean up. You write off losses. Humans included.

That's what the holiday ledger event was—clean-up.

I just made it worse on purpose.

You want the core of it?

I stopped being a witness and tested how much power I really had. Spoiler: too much.

CHAPTER 5
DANIEL

The year that mattered, business had been messy. There had been a raid on one of the warehouses. Two mid-level guys had flipped to save their own skins. A shipment had gone missing, and a few "associates" had died in car accidents that weren't really accidents.

By December, everyone was jumpy.

Mr. G wanted numbers tight. He didn't want any leaks or surprises.

In fact, he gave me clear instructions. "End of year, I want a clean ledger."

Clean meant a few things—no unexplained gaps, no phantom vendors, and no unpaid "loans."

We both knew what else it meant—anyone who cost more than they brought in needed to go.

He didn't say "killed," but he didn't need to. I'd been around long enough to know the code.

I went through every account, every bogus company, every shell, every name.

I made three piles—assets, liabilities, and a question mark.

The assets were simple. They were men who earned, people

who knew how to make trouble disappear, and fixers who could smooth things with cops or clerks.

The liabilities were also simple. They were drunks, gamblers, guys who liked to talk too much, and guys who had shown up in police reports one too many times.

Normally, I'd have handed those piles over and let them work it out.

The question mark was the gray area—names that needed more background done, names that I'd leave up to the boss to decide.

But that year, I did something different.

I started a fourth pile—people who frightened me.

Not because they had guns. Guns don't scare me, and let's face it, everyone around me had guns.

No, it was for people who frightened me because they were unpredictable.

The kind who might decide one night that they weren't afraid anymore. The kind who might walk into the office and shoot anyway. The kind who might take a ledger like mine and walk it into a precinct fifteen miles away.

They hadn't done anything wrong yet on paper. They were paid on time. They brought in enough. They didn't show up in incident reports.

But something about them rang wrong in my head.

One of them was that security guy who'd skimmed, the one I'd lied for. He'd stopped after the scare, but his eyes had changed. He watched Mr. G differently, and he watched me differently, almost like he was measuring us.

Another was a driver who'd been quiet for years then started asking questions about routes.

Then there was a consultant who kept checking how much life insurance coverage he had.

They weren't problems. Yet. But they were signals.

I could have flagged them as monitor or placed them in the question mark section. I could have stayed in my lane.

Instead, I decided to see what would happen if the ledger said they were liabilities.

I shifted numbers and moved dates. I reassigned certain short-falls and rolled some of the security guy's old skim into a current column.

I wrote three notes—chronic inefficiency, underperforming asset, and risk exceeds yield.

That's it. No blood. No drama.

I handed the file to Mr. G before Christmas. He glanced through it. He trusted my work. He always had.

He circled three names, the same three I'd added, and then he tapped the page.

"Write them off," he said.

Two days later, they were gone.

One died from a robbery at home, another one from a traffic collision, the last one from drug overdose.

I didn't check the scenes. I didn't need to.

I checked the books. The shortfalls vanished. The risk notes were satisfied. The ledger tightened.

The numbers were clean again.

That was my first taste of deliberate removal.

Not reaction. Not defense. Selection.

It felt… efficient.

Ugly word, I know, but it's the right one.

That's not the horror, though. The horror is what I did next.

I started doing it again.

Not every week. Not enough to draw attention but enough to test the edges.

Add a note. See who disappeared.

Take away a note. See who got a second chance.

I never directly wrote that someone needed to be killed, but again, I didn't have to.

All I did was tilt the scale on paper.

By the time Christmas came around the next year, I'd gotten

good at it. I made quiet adjustments, tiny changes that yielded big results.

That's what made the *holiday ledger event* possible, and why it was so goddamn easy for me to go through with it.

CHAPTER 6
DANIEL TO JACK

You're following, right? There's no question about who pulled triggers. You know that part isn't my concern. You're not stupid.

You've got your own version of this up here. The warden signs a form, someone gets moved, someone loses privileges, someone doesn't come back from a procedure.

Paper first. Action second.

So you get it.

You're probably wondering where this tips from evil accountant into full horror.

Here's your answer — I stopped just removing problems.

I used the ledger to erase an entire room.

On purpose.

At Christmas.

CHAPTER 7
DANIEL

We held holiday meetings every year. Stupid term if you ask me. All it meant was that everyone important had to show their face at least once in daylight, smile, drink something, and pretend we were a family.

Mr. G liked appearances. He said they kept things stable.

That year, the pressure was worse. Federal cases were creeping closer, and there was a rumor someone in the circle had turned and a rumor someone else was thinking about it.

Everyone looked fine on paper, intake good, losses contained, bribes paid, but the air had that charged feeling before a storm.

I went through the books before the meeting. Not just the numbers. I looked at the patterns too.

There were too many "exceptions." Too many "one-time favors." Too many side deals buried in petty cash.

I saw something no one else wanted to admit—we were rotting.

You can't put rot on a balance sheet, but you can put pressure.

I built a special page—end-of-year reconciliation. Nothing flashy. Just a compressed summary of liability.

I didn't assign it to individuals. Not this time. I assigned it to a core group.

I made sure every questionable thing done that year could be traced back to everyone in that room.

Shared risk. Shared exposure. Shared guilt.

I could have spread it out. I could have protected a few people.

Instead, I did the opposite.

I made sure I looked clean as glass. Every suspicious transfer, I pinned to the group along with every unaccounted bill, every double payment, every thin excuse.

On paper, they didn't just look sloppy. They looked dangerous.

Not dangerous to the public. Dangerous to Mr. G.

The holiday meeting was held in a back room of one of his clubs which basically ensured our privacy. Soundproofed more than you'd want to think about.

They all showed up—guys who'd worked for Mr. G for fifteen years, newer ones trying too hard to joke, people who thought I was just the man with the calculator.

I brought the binder. I opened to the reconciliation page. I laid it in front of him.

He read. His face didn't change.

It never did.

When he looked up, his eyes moved around the table, counting.

He didn't ask me to explain. He didn't ask who was at fault. He didn't ask if there was a way to fix it.

He just asked one thing. "How much of this comes back to you, Danny?"

I gave him the number. Zero.

He nodded, closed the file, and set his hand on it like he was blessing something. "Merry Christmas," he said.

He stood and walked out of the room.

For a few seconds, nothing happened. Some people made some jokes while others poured more drinks. Someone even made a crack about audits.

Then, the door clicked, and two of Mr. G's quiet men stepped in. The ones who didn't smile. The ones who didn't drink.

They locked the door.

I didn't stay. I didn't have to. Mr. G had already told me to go.

He'd patted the file before he'd stood. "You did good work," he'd said to me. "Go home to your family before the roads get bad. We'll handle the rest."

I knew what that meant. I walked to the door and waited for one of Mr. G's men to let me out. I walked away without looking back.

I drove past the club later that night just to see, you know? There were no sirens, no chaos. Just a dark building with its back entrance light off.

The next week, the books told the rest.

Half the liabilities vanished. So did half of the core group.

New names appeared. New positions were filled. On paper, the structure looked lighter. Stronger. Safer.

Mr. G called it pruning, but the feds called it something else when the bodies eventually surfaced.

I knew what it was. It wasn't just murder. It was a purge driven by my pen.

They didn't put that in the indictment. They called it the *holiday ledger event* because they couldn't wrap their heads around the idea that a man with a calculator and a neat handwriting had wiped out a room.

But I had. Not with bullets. With accounting.

That should have been my wake-up call.

It wasn't.

I kept working for another year. Cleaner books with fewer liabilities and more control.

Then someone talked. Not about the money. About the method.

Apparently, people pay attention when entire groups vanish while the accountant keeps cashing checks.

Investigators came. So did lawyers. Deals were made, and Mr. G traded pieces.

So did I.

They wanted testimony. I gave them just enough to keep breathing but not enough to give them the full story.

They never quite grasped how central I'd been. They thought I was a frightened little office rat trying to stay alive.

They weren't wrong, but they weren't completely right either.

The court called me "accessory by way of financial coordination." They looked at my health record. They looked at my breakdowns. They looked at the way I couldn't stop muttering numbers in holding.

Someone decided I wasn't fit for regular prison. Too fragile. Too cracked.

So they sent me here to this hellhole.

That's their mistake. They think this is a softer ending.

It isn't.

CHAPTER 8
DANIEL TO JACK

Now you know. I turned a Christmas meeting into a bloodbath without firing a shot. I wiped a room using columns and headings. I treated lives like overhead.

You believe I'm a monster? Good. You should.

But don't pretend you're different.

You carry a notebook. You decide who gets their story told, who gets recorded, and who gets left in the bed with nothing but a sheet over their face and a line in a file.

You're an auditor too, Jack. Different tools, same job.

You asked earlier… Well, you didn't, but you thought it—why did I ask if this would change the ending?

I'll tell you. I wanted to see if confession works like a write-off.

If I hand you the full picture, does the balance shift? Does the ledger change? Does whatever's waiting on the other side of all this give me partial credit for honesty?

My guess? No.

But I like clean books, so now mine are clean.

CHAPTER 9
JACK

Some men minimize. Some men justify. Daniel didn't bother. He laid his sins out in rows. Totals at the bottom. No rounding.

He wasn't proud. He wasn't remorseful in the way priests like to see. He was thorough.

"I just moved numbers," he says. "Everybody else decided what that meant."

"That's bullshit," I tell him.

He doesn't argue.

On the last night before Christmas, most people on this floor beg. They beg for time, for absolution, for someone they hurt to be okay.

Daniel doesn't beg. He just watches me like he's checking my math.

"You going to make it accurate?" he asks.

"All I do is write your story the way you tell it. Nothing else."

"Good," he says. "The truth's bad enough."

Outside his room, the ward hums in that thin way it does when everyone's trying to pretend the holiday matters. A nurse has a Santa hat on. The vents push lukewarm air. Someone down the hall coughs hard enough to rattle the rails.

Here's what I learned tonight. Some people kill with weapons. Some kill with neglect. Some kill with numbers.

On the way out, I pause at the nurses' station. There's a bowl of wrapped Christmas chocolate sitting here there. I take one, maybe two.

Christmas has never been my favorite season, but I stick the damn Santa hat on my head, pour some whiskey into my mug, and join Ike and the others by the tree.

Merry Christmas.

Jack

FINAL WRAP

Twelve nights.

Twelve rooms.

Twelve people who finally stopped fighting their own truths long enough to hand them over.

The decorations will come down tomorrow. The donation bin has already been dropped off, nice and full.

Most people think the Death Ward is about endings. They're wrong.

It's about inventory.

What people kept.

What they dropped.

What they couldn't carry into the last hour.

December makes those inventories honest.

If you've listened this far, then you understand something most people never will:

no one dies with the whole story on paper.

Someone has to stand in the room and hear the rest.

Thanks for being here.

Thanks for witnessing.

We'll clean up the lights. We'll reset the hallway. Life will get back to normal.

But for now —this was the Advent.

These were the twelve nights.

And I'll keep the rest the way I keep all of it: quiet, and exactly where it belongs.

Now ... let's move on to something fun. If you turn the page, I've included some paradoy christmas carols created right here on the Death Floor and there's even links so you can listen to them - which you should, just saying.

NEW HOLIDAY SONGS

- Merry Stichmas
- Frosty the Corpse Man
- Jingle Bones
- Twelve CC's of Christmas
- Run Run Orderly
- and more... (turn the page for some lyrics)

Want to listen to them all?

Listen via Asylum Radio: https://jacksteenbooks.com/asylum-radio/

or

Listen on SUNO: https://suno.com/@jacksteen

BLEACH BELLS

🎵 **BLEACH BELLS**
LINK TO LISTEN:
(Patreon-Ready Lyrics Block)
Bleach bells ring, are you listening?
Floors are white, bodies glistening.
A horrible sight,
we're happy tonight—
working in a Death Ward wonderland.
Down the hall, something's humming,
sounds like joy… or death incoming.
But don't you fear—
just smile, my dear,
we're living in a Death Ward wonderland.
In the morgue, we'll build a snowman,
made of sheets and toe tags, neat and clean.
He'll ask, *"Am I alive?"* and we'll say *"No, man—*
just rest tight till Jack begins the scene."
Night shift sings while we're sweeping,
and the walls pretend they're sleeping.
We'll mop till dawn,

pretend nothing's wrong—
it's Christmas in a Death Ward wonderland.

FROSTY THE CORPSE MAN

♫ FROSTY THE CORPSE MAN
LINK TO LISTEN:
Frosty the Corpse Man
was a body cold and gray,
with a scalpel nose
and toes that froze
the night they took him away.
There must have been some magic
in that IV bag they found,
for when we stuck it in his vein—
he screamed and turned around!
Frosty the Corpse Man
stared at us with vacant eyes.
He said, *"Who turned out the lights?"*
and gave the tech a fright—
we assumed he'd stay deceased, surprise!
His jaw unhinged so slowly,
like he had a joke to tell,
but the only sound that left his throat
was the morgue's old freezer bell.
Oh, Frosty...

He shuffled down the hallway, stiff as ice,
and asked us for a coat.
We said, *"Corpse Man, not tonight —*
you're better staying cold."
Frosty the Corpse Man
wandered near the nurse's bay,
left a little trail of frost
and a sense of something lost
in the charts he stole away.
We chased him toward the stairwell,
shouting, *"Sir, you can't just roam!"*
But he waved goodbye with a brittle hand—
and froze right back to stone.
Frosty the Corpse Man,
he'll be sleeping where he fell.
So zip him up tight,
and wish him goodnight—
the morgue keeps secrets well.

JINGLE BONES

♫ JINGLE BONES
  LINK TO LISTEN:

Jingle bones, jingle bones,
  rattling down the hall—
  somebody left the morgue unlocked,
  now he's having a ball!
  Jingle bones, jingle bones,
  clattering on the tile.
  You'd scream too
  if you suddenly knew
  he's been walking for a while!
  Bones in the air, bones on the floor,
  bones in the linen chute—
  we'll pick 'em up
  and stitch him back
  with sutures and a hoot!
  Jingle bones, jingle bones,
  laugh until you drop—
  he shakes his hips
  and his pelvis slips—

someone call the mop!
Nurses duck, orderlies cheer—
holiday mayhem's here.
He taps his ribs like a xylophone
to spread some festive fear.
The Warden yells, "Contain him!"
but Frosty's cousin won't obey—
he rattles past with a jaunty laugh
and jingles all the way!
Patient: *rattle-rattle!*
Jack: "Stop right there."
Patient: *clickity-clack!*
Jack: "Don't you dare."
Patient: *tap-tap-tap!*
Jack: "Okay, that's fair—
at least he's in the holiday spirit."
Jingle bones, jingle bones,
echo through the night—
even ghosts lean out to grin
and judge his shaky gait.
Jingle bones, jingle bones,
spin 'em like a top—
he'll dance 'til dawn
then fall apart—
and that's when we clock off.

THE TWELVE CC'S OF CHRISTMAS

♫ THE TWELVE CC'S OF CHRISTMAS

LINK TO LISTEN:

On the first night of Christmas, my patient gave to me—
 a chart I was afraid to read.
 On the second night of Christmas, my patient gave to me—
 two missing meds,
 and a chart I was afraid to read.
 On the third night of Christmas, my patient gave to me—
 three coded beeps,
 two missing meds,
 and a chart I was afraid to read.
 On the fourth night of Christmas—
 four false alarms…
 FIIIIIVE CC's TOO MUCH!
 Six syringes empty,
 seven nurses shouting,
 eight shifts of chaos,
 nine gurneys rolling,

ten interns crying,
eleven doctors guessing,
twelve CC's of something...
...and a chart I was afraid to read.

UP ON THE HOUSETOP
(THE PATIENT CRAWLS)

♫ UP ON THE HOUSETOP (THE PATIENT CRAWLS)

LINK TO LISTEN:

Up on the housetop the patient crawls,
    nail-scratched fingers on concrete walls.
    Down through the vents comes a raspy laugh—
    someone forgot to check his chart and path!
    Ho-ho-ho—what do you know?
    Up on the housetop he won't go!
    Creeps and crawls through every hall,
    catch him before he tries to call…
    Through the ducts he twists with glee,
    muttering secrets meant for me.
    Nurses scream, "He's loose again!"
    Orderlies chase him with a pen.
    Ho-ho-ho—stop, don't be slow!
    He found the morgue and said hello!
    Creeps and crawls through every hall,
    laughing like he owns it all…
    Patient: *scratch-scratch-scratch!*

Jack: "That's not a cat."
Patient: *tap-tap-tap!*
Jack: "Put the tiles back."
Patient: *hiss-hiss-hiss!*
Jack: "Nope, I'm done with this—
at least try crawling toward your room."
Up on the rooftop he waves at me,
grin too wide for a human to be.
"Come on, Jack, the view's divine—
the ward looks pretty when it's night-time."
Ho-ho-ho—I tell him no!
"Get off the roof before you go!"
But down he leaps with a feral call—
landed soft as snow… somehow still tall.
Up on the housetop he crawled tonight—
write that in the incident write.
I'll sign my name with a weary scrawl…
and pray tomorrow no one crawls.

HAVE YOURSELF A
CLINICAL CHRISTMAS

🎵 HAVE YOURSELF A CLINICAL CHRISTMAS

LINK TO LISTEN:

Have yourself a clinical Christmas,
 let your pulse be light.
 From now on your charting
 might be shorter than tonight.
 Have yourself a typical Christmas,
 with the usual scares—
 vitals low, the lights flicker slow,
 ghosts pace in pairs.
 Here we are in the endless shift,
 slogging through the snow.
 Patients cheer with a hollow grin—
 none of them can go.
 Through the years we all end up here,
 if we make it far.
 Truth be told, the Death Ward's really
 Christmas's last star.
 So whisper me your symptoms,

your secrets, and your sins.
I'll write them in this notebook
before the night begins.
Have yourself a clinical Christmas,
keep your heartbeat slow.
If you hear the footsteps in the hall,
pretend they already know.

SILENT NIGHT SHIFT

🎵 **SILENT NIGHT SHIFT**

LINK TO LISTEN:

Silent night, shift of night,
    all is dim, no working light.
    Only the monitors humming their tune,
    soft little beeps in a dying room—
    sleep in shadows and fear,
    sleep in shadows and fear.
    Silent ward, voices stored,
    whispers cling like prayers ignored.
    I walk the halls with a chart held tight,
    hoping the ghosts leave me alone tonight—
    still they follow me near,
    still they follow me near.
    Silent plea: "Stay with me,"
    patient eyes on eternity.
    I take his hand as the cold creeps in,
    promise I'll write what he can't begin—
    truth no one wants to hear,

truth no one wants to hear.
Silent shift, small last gift,
breath grows thin, the soul starts to lift.
He whispers, "Was it all a dream?"
I tell him, "Rest. You're warm, it seems…"
even if death is near,
even if death is near.

MERRY STITCHMAS

🎵 **MERRY STITCHMAS**

LINK TO LISTEN:

We wish you a Merry Stitchmas,
    we wish you a Merry Stitchmas,
    we wish you a Merry Stitchmas—
    from OR Three.
    Good sutures we bring,
    for patients and things—
    now hold still a moment,
    this *might* start to sting.
    We're stitching and switching,
    tying and twitching,
    hoping this edging
    will stop all the drip.
    So hand me the needle,
    the sharp one (not legal),
    the one the Warden
    said, *"Jack, don't let people —*
    see you with that."

Oh bring us some sterile swabs,
oh bring us some sterile swabs—
and a coffee, please.
We won't go until we stitch right,
we won't go until we stitch right—
it's Merry Stitchmas Eve.
So pass the thread and tie the knot,
ignore the voice that says, "That's not—
how wounds are closed," but what do they know?
I learned from ghosts; they sew so slow.
Now tuck in the edges neatly,
and hum something vaguely sweetly—
pray that it holds completely
through Christmas night.
We wish you a Merry Stitchmas,
your skin looks delicious—
I mean *ambitious,*
don't worry,
you're stitched up tight.